THE KILLINGS
AT
COYOTE SPRINGS

THE KILLINGS
AT
COYOTE SPRINGS

LEWIS B. PATTEN

DOUBLEDAY & COMPANY, INC.

GARDEN CITY, NEW YORK

1977

All the characters in this book are fictitious,
and any resemblance to actual persons, living or dead,
is purely coincidental.

ISBN: 0-385-12668-9
Library of Congress Catalog Card Number 76–24213
Copyright © 1977 by Lewis B. Patten
All rights reserved
Printed in the United States of America
First Edition

THE KILLINGS
AT
COYOTE SPRINGS

CHAPTER 1

Because he knew the twice-weekly arrival of the stagecoach was an event for both the kids and the adults of Coyote Springs, Red Holbrook, the driver, cracked his whip over the heads of the lead team and loosed a yell as the coach rattled over the bridge at the edge of town. The horses lunged against their collars and broke into a gallop despite their weariness. Careening and lurching, the coach raced noisily up the street, raising a cloud of dust that rolled over and past it when it was hauled to a stop in front of the three-story Colorado Hotel.

Two passengers were inside the coach. One, Frank Cole, was big, six feet two inches tall, weighing two hundred pounds and none of it fat. He uncoiled himself and eased out the coach door, which seemed too small for him. He stood in the settling yellow dust, peering around, stretching out the kinks put into his body by the long haul from the last way station and by the cramped interior of the coach.

The second man, as different from Cole as night from

day, stepped briskly out behind him, brushing dust from his black serge coat. He was a good eight inches shorter than was Cole. His skin was pale, as though he spent most of his time indoors. He was a little plump and there was a soft look to him that immediately told anyone who saw him that he did no work with his hands.

Holbrook handed down Cole's ragged carpetbag and the other man's worn alligator grip. He exchanged mail sacks with a gaunt man wearing a green eyeshade and gold-rimmed spectacles who, after a glance at the two passengers, hurried away. Holbrook climbed stiffly down, tossed nickels to two boys who were holding the bridles of the lead team, and went into the hotel bar for a beer. Cole glanced at his traveling companion. "Can I buy you a beer, Mr. Flagg?"

Joel Flagg nodded, and preceded him into the hotel. The bartender already had served the driver. Cole raised two fingers. The bartender drew two large mugs of beer, raked the heads off with a stick, and slid them down the bar. Cole raised his to Flagg. "Luck."

The other nodded. "I think we'll need it," he said.

Cole gulped half the mug of beer without taking it from his mouth, and afterward wiped the foam off his wide mustache with the back of a hand. He wore tan canvas pants, down-at-the-heel Texas boots, and a blue shirt darkened with sweat down the front and underneath his arms. Over his shirt was a vest that most times hid the U.S. marshal's badge that was pinned to the pocket of his shirt.

He finished the beer and waited for the other man to finish his. Then he asked, "Want to hire a rig and go out there or would you rather check into the hotel and rest a while?"

"I want to go out there right away."

Joel Flagg was a reporter for the *Rocky Mountain News*. He knew this was going to be the biggest story he had ever covered, and he still didn't know how he was going to handle it. Four months before, Colonel George Armstrong Custer and 225 men of his command had been wiped out by the Sioux at the Little Big Horn, and he didn't think four months had cooled the country's fury over it. His coverage of this story was more likely to end his career than further it. But Flagg was an honest man and he would do the best he could no matter who got hurt.

He finished his beer, sweating now. He dragged a handkerchief from his pocket, took off his derby hat, and mopped his streaming forehead. He said, "All right. Let's go."

Cole put two nickels on the bar, then carried his carpetbag into the lobby. He put it down in front of the desk. He signed the register and told the clerk to put the bag in his room. Flagg followed suit. Cole led the way out into the brilliant October sunlight, glanced up and down the street to locate the livery barn, and then headed toward it.

The livery barn was the same pale yellow as the hotel. It sagged slightly and was missing a good many shingles from its roof. Some had been replaced with straightened-out tin cans, now red with rust, but it was obvious that no repairs had been made recently. A wooden ramp led into the stable from the street.

Inside, on the right, there was a tack room and office. A man stood up and came out of it as Cole and Flagg came in. He was dirty and unshaven and shuffled along with his shoulders stooped. He asked, "Whatcha need?"

Cole said, "A buckboard and team."

The man nodded. He shuffled toward the rear, led first one horse and then another out of their stalls. He brought both to the front and began to throw harness onto one of them. Cole harnessed the other. Finished, the stableman backed them into place in front of a buckboard and hitched them up. He asked, "How long you want it for?"

"Couple of hours, I guess. Where's that Indian camp?"

The stableman swallowed twice and licked his lips. Cole said, "I'll find out from somebody. You'd just as well tell me and save a lot of trouble." He pushed his vest aside so that the stableman could see his marshal's badge.

The stableman's voice came out as shrill as a boy's. "It's out . . ." He stopped and cleared his throat, then continued in a more normal tone. "It's down across the bridge the same way the stage came in. Turn right after you cross the bridge. There's wagon tracks to follow and they'll lead you to it."

"How far?"

"Half a dozen miles, I guess."

Cole climbed to the buckboard seat. Flagg climbed up on the other side. Cole drove the team down the ramp and out into the street. The stage was just pulling away from the hotel, turning in the middle of the street to head for the livery barn and a change of horses. It was early afternoon. Everyone on the street was watching Cole and Flagg.

Cole drove down the street toward the bridge at its lower end. He had been a law officer for a good many years and in that time had developed an ability to sense the mood of a person or a place. The mood of this place was hostile and afraid. He could feel it in the stares of the people on the street. He had felt it in the stableman.

He turned his head and glanced at Flagg, immediately knowing that Flagg had felt it too.

Cole had no idea what they were going to find when they reached their destination. The information received at the U.S. marshal's office in Denver had been too vague.

All he knew was that there had been a killing or killings at an Indian camp near the town of Coyote Springs.

The buckboard rattled across the bridge. Beneath the bridge the creek was a trickle less than two feet wide, but its bed, twenty feet wide with steep banks on both sides, told Cole it carried a lot of water in the spring or after a heavy rain.

Tall cottonwoods and willows lined the creek, their leaves bright gold in the early-afternoon sun.

Cole glanced at Flagg. The man seemed unusually pale. His hands were clenched on his knees and his back was rigid and tense. Unexpectedly, Flagg turned his head and said, "It's too damn pretty here for what we're going to find."

"Maybe it won't be that bad."

"I hope not."

"Maybe there's nothing left. Maybe it's all been cleaned up."

"If it has we'll have a hell of a time getting anybody to admit anything."

Cole felt no particular dread of what they might find at the site of the Indian camp. He had seen dead bodies before. He had been through the war, emerging at its end a captain of cavalry. He had seen long-dead and bloated bodies stacked against a stone wall like logs because the fighting had been too hot for anybody to bury them. What he would see at the Indian village could be no worse.

The horses traveled at a steady trot. Because of the roughness of the two-track lane, the buckboard bounded back and forth and up and down, but the spring seat spared its occupants the worst of the jolting. The miles fell behind.

The creek wound back and forth, snakelike across the rolling plain. The road, however, straightened out most of the sharp bends in it. A breeze blew toward the pair.

They smelled the Indian camp long before they brought it into sight. The smell was the sickish, sweet smell of rotting flesh.

A couple of dozen vultures rose as the buckboard made a turn and Cole brought the Indian camp into sight. It wasn't much. No tipis. There were a couple of brush shelters and three lean-tos made of tattered canvas. A quarter mile away a few horses grazed.

The buckboard horses, sighting something, balked. One of them reared and tried to turn. Cole turned them aside, drove them to the nearest tree. He got down and tied one of the horses to the tree with a piece of rope he found lying in the back of the rig.

Afoot, then, he and Flagg walked toward the Indian camp. The vultures were now circling overhead.

Cole had thought nothing he could see there would be worse than what he had seen during the war. He had been wrong.

The first body he came upon was that of a youngster who could not have been more than ten or eleven years old. Not much was left. The boy's abdominal cavity had been torn open by the vultures and most of his face was gone. Only clothing, itself partially shredded, told Cole the body was that of a boy.

He glanced at Flagg. The man's face was greenish gray. He felt Cole's glance on him and made a sickly smile. Then, suddenly, he turned and bolted for the trees. Cole heard him vomiting.

He went on past the boy. Inside the nearest lean-to, untouched by the vultures because they probably had feared the flapping canvas, lay the body of a woman. Beside the woman was a baby that couldn't have been more than six months old. Blood had stained the clothing of the baby. It had literally drenched that of the woman, telling Cole she must have been shot at least half a dozen times.

Both bodies were bloated, but even with the bloating Cole could tell how emaciated they had been in life. He felt his own stomach churn, and turned his head to look for Flagg.

The reporter stood at the edge of the trees, his face shining with sweat, the color of his skin still greenish gray. Cole called, "Come over here."

Anger was stirring in him now, because it was becoming obvious that what had happened here had been cold-blooded butchery. He had yet to see a weapon, and certainly this starving, desperately poor group of Indians could have been no threat to anyone.

Flagg walked unsteadily to where he stood. He looked at the two bodies inside the lean-to and quickly looked away. Cole walked on. He found an old man next, torn by the vultures the way the boy had been, and then a younger man, perhaps his own age, whose face was, for some reason, nearly intact.

Besides these five, he found four more bodies, one of a young woman, one of a middle-aged woman, another boy, and a man that appeared to have been around forty years

old although it was hard to tell because of the way his face
had been eaten by the vultures.

By now, Cole himself was sick. Pale and shaking, Flagg
glanced at him and said, "I can't stand any more. I got to
get away from here." His voice was weak and trembling.

Cole still had not seen a weapon. He stood upwind of
the last body he had found and watched Flagg hurry back
toward the buckboard. Reaching it, Flagg draped himself
over one of the wheels and vomited again.

The lack of weapons didn't, of course, mean that the Indians hadn't had any. They could have been taken by the
men who had done the killing, along with whatever other
artifacts the Indians might have had. There couldn't have
been much in the way of loot though, Cole thought. These
Indians had been too desperately poor.

He didn't know enough about Indians to tell what tribe
they had belonged to. They might be Cheyenne, but they
were probably Arapaho. In this area, anyway.

He left the bodies and made a big circle of the pitiful little camp. He found plenty of horse tracks, but too much
time had passed to identify any of them. He couldn't even
tell for sure if the animals making them had been shod.

He returned to the buckboard. Flagg's face shone with
sweat and still looked green. Cole untied the horse and
climbed to the buckboard seat. "Let's go. We've seen all
we need to see for now."

Nine dead Indians, he thought. Three of them women.
One a baby and two young boys. All emaciated. All starving. They must have camped here without knowing they
were so close to a white man's town.

Someone must have discovered them and carried news of

their presence into town. The people, angry over what had happened to Custer at the Little Big Horn, had ridden out and murdered them for revenge.

No, he thought. Not all the people of the town. Only a few. And now his job was to find those few.

Maybe no jury in Colorado would convict them for what they'd done. Maybe feeling against Indians still ran too high.

But he had to try. His duty and his own sense of outrage demanded that.

CHAPTER 2

All the way back to town, Cole held the buckboard team to a steady trot. Flagg was silent, but as the fresh, winy air cleared the stench from his lungs, he began to regain his normal color, which, while pale, was not such a sickly shade as before.

Neither man spoke for a long time. At last, near the place where the road crossed the bridge, Flagg muttered, "The sons of bitches! How the hell could they do it? Kids, and women and a baby, too!"

Cole shrugged, thinking the same thing himself. He drove across the bridge and up the main street. This time, nobody looked at them. The fact that they did not was as revealing as their stares had been earlier.

Cole halted the buckboard in front of the livery stable. He climbed down and went inside. The hostler was in the tack room, but Cole had heard him scurrying and knew he had been watching them from the dark interior of the livery barn. Cole asked, "You got a photographer in town?"

The hostler shook his head fearfully. Cole said bluntly,

"If I find out you're lying, you can be charged as an accessory after the fact."

The hostler's knees had begun to shake. Cole said, "I'll ask once more. Is there a photographer in town?"

The hostler nodded.

"Where's he live?"

"Straight up this street. Last house on the right at the upper end of town."

Cole asked, "What's *your* name?"

"Ed Donovan."

Cole nodded shortly and left. He climbed to the buckboard seat and drove straight up the street, looking neither to right nor left. By now the street was completely deserted except for a dog scratching himself in the shade of the Brundage Mercantile.

The house to which they had been directed was a single story, its front yard surrounded by a white picket fence. A huge maple tree shaded the front yard, its leaves both gold and orange.

There was a sign in the front window that read LUCAS ORANGE, PHOTOGRAPHER. Cole halted the buckboard and went through the gate and up the path to the porch. A sign on the door said COME IN, so he did. There were several large cameras and related equipment. There was a backdrop against the wall depicting a garden with carefully tended lawn and a winding path. A man was standing in a doorway leading back to the rest of the house.

He was built much like Flagg, short and plump and soft. His skin was tanned, however, in contrast to Flagg's pallid one. Cole asked, "You Lucas Orange?"

The man nodded.

Cole said, "I'm Frank Cole, U.S. marshal from Denver. I want you to bring your camera and take some pictures down at that Indian camp."

Orange's face lost color now, and his eyes looked like those of a trapped animal. Cole said, "Now."

"I'm busy now. Maybe tomorrow." Orange's expression was hopeful, as if he wished Cole would accept his excuse and go away, while all the time knowing he would not.

Cole said, "Now. And when we get back, I'm going to stand right here while you develop your photographs. So do it right the first time and we won't have to go back out there again."

Orange hesitated a moment more, looking for some sign of relenting in Cole's face. He didn't find it. Cole was remembering the way all those bodies had looked and wondering if Orange had been one of those responsible. Finally Orange turned away and, hands trembling, began to gather the equipment he would need. It was bulky and heavy, and Cole helped him carry it out to the rig. Orange spread a worn blanket in the back of the buckboard and laid his camera on that. Then he folded the blanket carefully over the camera.

Flagg moved over to the middle of the seat and Orange climbed up. Cole said, "Mr. Flagg, this is Mr. Orange, the photographer. He's going to take some photographs out at the Indian camp for us."

Flagg stuck out his hand and Orange shook it without enthusiasm. Weakly he asked, "Are you from the marshal's office too?"

"No. I'm a reporter for the *Rocky Mountain News*."

Orange had begun to sweat. As they passed the Colorado Hotel, Cole turned his head and looked directly at him. "Were you in on that thing out at the Indian camp?"

He thought Orange was going to choke. The man had to swallow twice before he could speak. "No sir. No sir! I sure didn't have anything to do with that!"

The street was still deserted, but Cole could see faces peering out from windows all up and down the street. The dog got up from the shade of the store and walked halfway out into the street, wagging his tail tentatively.

Down across the bridge Cole went, and took the right turn into the wagon ruts. Orange sweated helplessly for a while. Finally he shifted around on the seat so he could get at the handkerchief in his hip pocket. He dragged it out and mopped his streaming face.

The wind must have changed in the past hour, because they saw the Indian camp this time before smelling it. The vultures were tearing at the bodies again. They rose as the buckboard approached, their flapping thunderous in the nearly complete silence of the place.

Cole drove the team to the same tree where he had tied before. He tied one horse to the tree. Orange was looking fearfully toward the Indian camp. Cole said, "They're dead. They won't hurt you. Bring your stuff and I'll tell you what I want pictures of."

He led the photographer to the body of the first boy. Orange stood there staring, seemingly unable to put his camera down. Cole said, "Take a picture of him. Hurry up. There are a lot more to take and the light isn't going to last."

Dazedly, Orange set his camera up. He went through the motions automatically, focusing, finally clicking the shutter. Cole said, "Take two of each. Just to be sure."

Orange took a second photograph of the boy. Cole said, "Come on," and led him to the shelter in which the woman and baby were. He said, "You'll need a flash to take this one."

Orange rigged the flash. The powder went off with a blinding flash, sending up a dense white cloud of smoke. Cole had him take a second one and then led him to the body of the old man, the young one, and successively, the other four. At each, Orange took two photographs. When he was finished, he was sick. He left his camera and ran to some brush, where he deposited the contents of his stomach on the ground. He came back pale and sweating, and Cole asked, "You think you have them all?"

Orange nodded without speaking.

"I want you to be sure. If you didn't get them and somebody comes out here and destroys the evidence, you may end up on trial along with the ones who did the killing."

Weakly Orange said, "I got the pictures. I'm sure of it."

"Then, let's go back to town and develop them." Cole strode back to the buckboard, followed by Flagg. Orange brought up the rear.

The drive back to Coyote Springs was made in silence. At the edge of town, Orange finally voiced what was in his mind. "What are you going to do? To the men that killed those Indians?"

"Find 'em first." The rig rattled across the bridge and up the street.

"And when you do?"

Cole turned his head and looked at the photographer. His eyes were grayish, or maybe a light brown. They made the photographer feel cold. Cole asked, "It was murder, wasn't it?"

"But. . . ." Orange stopped.

Cole knew what he had been going to say. That they were only Indians and what was all the fuss about? Cole said, "But what? They were only Indians?"

"I didn't mean. . . ."

Cole shrugged. "Never mind." It wasn't fair to take out his anger on this photographer. He hadn't been in on what had happened back there at the Indian camp.

Orange finally managed to say, "It's what happened to Custer a few months ago."

"Those people out there had nothing to do with what happened to Custer. They don't even belong to the same tribe."

It was different driving up the street this time. It looked like the whole town was out. They lined the street, staring with silent animosity at the buckboard and the three men on the seat.

Cole stared back coldly. He wasn't an easy man to scare. But the impact of all those hostile stares was almost physical.

The buckboard rattled on up the street, and Cole finally drew it to a halt in front of Orange's house. He got down, tied to the hitching post, then helped Orange and Flagg carry the equipment in.

He stared out the window into the street as Orange went to work in a small room adjoining the one where he usually took his photographs. Flagg sat down in one of the straight-backed chairs, while Cole impatiently paced the floor. For a long time, neither man spoke.

Finally Flagg asked, "What's next?"

"That's about it for today."

"And tomorrow?"

"I'll hire some men and go out and bury the bodies."

"What if you can't hire any men?"

"Then I'll do it myself."

Flagg was silent for a moment. Then he said, "Did you see the way they looked at us as we drove up the street?"

"I saw."

"It gave me the shivers. You don't think they'll try getting rid of us?"

"I doubt it. They wouldn't dare touch a U.S. marshal."

But he wasn't sure. The hostility in the people's stares as they drove up the street had been too real.

Flagg asked, "Do you think it was because of Custer?"

"Partly, maybe. People were pretty stirred up when the news first came out. But there had to be more to it than that. Hell, Custer was killed in June."

"How do you think the people in Denver will react when my story comes out?"

Cole stopped pacing and looked at him. "Depends on how you write your story, I suppose." He studied Flagg for several moments. "You got sick out there, but how do you really feel about what happened to those people? Are they 'only Indians' to you or were they a bunch of half-starved, homeless travelers that got themselves butchered for somebody's sport?"

Flagg's face colored slightly, but his glance didn't waver from Cole's. "I'm here to tell what happened and you're here to see that their killers pay for killing them."

Orange came into the room. "The prints are drying. They'll be ready in half an hour."

Cole said, "We'll wait." He knew the minute he and Flagg left the photographer's half a dozen or more of the town's residents would descend on him.

Orange said hopefully, "I could bring them down to the hotel."

Frank Cole shook his head. "No hurry. We've got plenty of time." He knew what Orange was hoping for—that he and Flagg would leave, giving those guilty of the killings a chance to get their hands on the photographs and the negative plates. With those destroyed, the other evidence could also be destroyed, by fire, during the night. By morning there wouldn't be any evidence.

He had told Flagg there was no danger, but he didn't believe that himself. Desperate men are capable of desperate things. And the killers of those Indians must certainly be desperate.

They would reason that if they got rid of Cole and Flagg and destroyed the photographs and physical evidence, they'd at least be no worse off than they were right now.

And, reluctantly, Cole had to admit that they were right. Bodies could be hidden successfully. In two weeks, that Indian camp could completely disappear.

Orange finally brought the photographs. Cole studied each one, with Flagg looking over his shoulder. Then, slipping them into the brown envelope Orange had given him, he got to his feet. Orange's price for them was four dollars. Cole paid him and went outside.

The sun was setting, and the thin clouds overhead were a blazing gold that put a warm glow over the town. Cole climbed to the buckboard seat, reached down a hand to assist Flagg, then drove down the street toward the livery barn.

He dropped Flagg off at the hotel and returned the rig himself. He paid for it and walked back toward the hotel.

It was dusk by now. The streets were nearly deserted. But Cole could feel eyes watching him.

CHAPTER 3

Flagg had disappeared when Cole entered the lobby of the hotel. He crossed to the desk for his key.

There was a new desk clerk on duty—thin, bespectacled, and middle-aged. Cole asked, "What room did you put me in?"

"Seven, Mr. Cole." The clerk handed him a key.

Cole turned, nearly bumping into a man that had come up behind him.

"Mr. Cole? I'm Carl Brundage. Can I talk to you?"

Cole shrugged. "Why not?"

"How about the bar? We can have a drink."

Cole followed him into the hotel bar. Brundage went to a corner table, and both men sat down. Brundage was a portly, florid-faced man, perhaps sixty years old. There was a look of substance to him, in the way he dressed, in the expression in his eyes. He was obviously a man used to receiving the respect of the community, used to giving orders and having them obeyed. Cole recalled that the mercantile store had borne the name Brundage, but he was willing to bet the store wasn't all that Brundage owned in Coyote Springs.

Brundage beckoned the bartender, and when he arrived at the table, glanced at Cole. "What's your pleasure, Mr. Cole?"

"Whiskey will do," Cole said.

The bartender withdrew and returned immediately with a bottle and two glasses. The whiskey brand told Cole this was probably Brundage's private stock. Brundage poured a couple of fingers into Cole's glass, a similar amount into his own. He raised the glass. "Your health."

Cole grinned faintly, but he drank and put down the glass. "What's on your mind, Mr. Brundage?"

"I understand you're here to investigate that deplorable thing down at the Indian camp."

"I am."

"Would you mind telling me who sent for you?"

"I mind."

Brundage seemed to have expected his refusal. "What are you going to do?"

"Find the men responsible."

"Do you think any jury would convict them? Considering what happened at the Little Big Horn a couple of months ago?"

Cole shrugged. "That's not my concern. That's the business of the courts."

Brundage said, "I don't suppose there's any way. . . ." He paused, and carefully avoided looking at Frank Cole. When Cole said nothing, Brundage went on, "Something like this can ruin a town. I understand you brought a reporter along with you. If something like this gets splashed across the front page of the *Rocky Mountain News.* . . ."

Cole looked him straight in the eye. "Have you been down to that Indian camp, Mr. Brundage?"

"No. I. . . ."

"You ought to go. Maybe then you wouldn't be trying so hard to bribe me not to do what I was sent down here to do."

Brundage's face flushed angrily. His eyes turned as hard as bits of slate. He got abruptly to his feet. "You are dead wrong, Mr. Cole. I wasn't trying to bribe you. I made no mention of money."

"Didn't have to. I'm not a fool."

"I think you are a fool, Mr. Cole. I just hope you don't end up a dead fool before this is over with."

Cole stared coolly up at him. "Attempted bribes. Then threats. Be careful, Mr. Brundage."

"You are the one who should be careful, Mr. Cole." He snatched his bottle from the table and strode to the bar. He nearly broke it banging it down on the top of the bar.

Cole got to his feet. He went back into the lobby and climbed the stairs to his room. If he'd had any illusions before, he had none left. Both he and Flagg were in danger here, and would be until their investigation was over with.

He unlocked his room and stepped inside. His carpetbag was on the bed. Suddenly very conscious of the envelope of photographs in his hand, he stared around the room, looking for a hiding place.

He saw none where the photographs would not be found if someone should search the room. Then his glance touched the window shade.

The room was almost dark and it was nearly dark outside. Swiftly he crossed the room, climbed on a chair, and, standing to one side of the window as he did so, removed the window shade from the brackets holding it. He put it down on the floor, unrolled it, then took out the photographs and, one by one, laid them on the window shade at the upper end, near the roller.

Now, carefully, he rerolled the shade and studied it critically in the faint light coming in the window. No telltale bulge showed where the photographs were, probably because he had put them in place one by one and not in a bunch.

He climbed on the chair and replaced the shade. He pulled it part-way down, pleased that the photographs still did not show. There appeared to be enough shade to pull it all the way down without letting the photographs fall out.

He crossed the room now and lighted the lamp. He put the envelope that had contained the photographs in his carpetbag.

There was a knock on the door. Cole got his revolver out of his carpetbag. He opened the door.

Flagg stood just outside. "You had anything to eat?"

Cole shook his head.

"Shall we go down?"

Cole nodded. "All right." He turned, got gun belt and holster out of the carpetbag and strapped them around his waist. He thrust the revolver down into the holster after first checking its loads. Flagg asked, "What's that for?"

"I was approached by the town's leading citizen, Mr. Brundage. He tried to bribe me, and when that didn't work, threatened me."

"You don't think they'll actually try anything?"

"I know they will."

Flagg looked scared. Cole said, "They'll probably go

after me first." He led the way down the stairs and across the lobby to the door leading into the hotel dining room. The place was jammed and every table was taken. Cole glanced at Flagg. "Want a drink before dinner? Maybe by the time we get back there'll be room for us."

Flagg nodded. Cole said, "There's a saloon down the street called the Drovers. Sound all right?"

Flagg nodded, obviously still shaken by the threat that had been made against Cole. They went out of the hotel, crossed the veranda, and descended the steps to the walk.

Cole could see the Drovers Saloon from the walk in front of the hotel. Horses were racked solidly in front of it. There were a lot of people on the street, all of whom managed to avoid looking directly either at Cole or at Flagg. Cole had the feeling, however, that as soon as they had passed, everyone stared closely at them.

He headed toward the saloon, with Flagg keeping pace. Softly, so as not to be overheard, Flagg asked, "What did you do with the photographs?"

"Hid them."

"Where?"

"Someplace where they won't be found."

"For God's sake, man, don't you even trust me?"

"The fewer people who know, the safer they're going to be."

That statement seemed to upset Flagg even more, because the implication was that those guilty of the killings out at the Indian camp might try to torture the information out of them. He said, "I don't know whether I'm the man for this job or not. I've never even been in a fist fight. Not in my whole damn life."

Cole didn't want to lecture Flagg, but he knew the man needed some bolstering. He said, "There are all kinds of courage. Man isn't necessarily born with it."

"Isn't he?"

"No. And don't get the idea that courage means not being afraid. It don't. I went up the hill at Gettysburg when more than anything else in the world I wanted to turn around and run the other way."

"You don't mean to tell me that everybody felt that way?"

"I don't know what everybody felt."

"Aren't there men who just plainly aren't afraid?"

Cole shrugged. "Maybe. I've heard so. But I figure the ones who aren't afraid are too stupid to feel anything. Hell, man, fear was put into man and animals to help keep them alive. It's like pain. If you burn your hand, you've got sense enough, or instinct enough, to pull it back out of the fire. The same applies to courage. I always figured men have the most real, raw courage of any animal because a man will do things he knows are dangerous just because he thinks they're right. Show me an animal that operates on any principle like that."

They had nearly reached the Drovers Saloon. Flagg looked at Cole gratefully. He said, "Thanks. You made me feel better."

Cole said, "Hell, you wouldn't even be here if you didn't have guts. You knew it was a murder investigation when you came down here. And whenever there's murder, there's danger to whoever investigates."

They paused at the entrance to the Drovers Saloon. The windows were dirty and didn't look as if they had been washed for months. There was a panel of stained, leaded glass over the two swinging doors depicting a rather crude nude woman in a reclining position. The doors themselves were louvered, part doors for use in warm weather, and swung back into a closed position when they were released.

This saloon was as crowded as the bar at the hotel, but there was enough space at the bar for two. Cole pushed his way toward it through a crowd that was deliberately slow to make way for them. There was some muttering as he jostled various individuals, but nothing more than muttering. Flagg stayed immediately behind Cole, looking nervous if not outright scared.

Cole reached the bar and Flagg took the place beside him. Cole waited a moment while the bartender deliberately ignored him. Then he picked up an empty beer mug and banged it down thunderously on the bar.

The bartender started and glanced at him. Cole said pleasantly, "Two whiskeys."

The bartender, muscular and bald and with a wide mustache, nodded curtly. He brought a bottle and two glasses. He put the glasses down in front of the two men and uncorked the bottle.

As he got it uncorked, it seemed to slip out of his hand. It landed on its side on the bar in front of Cole, neck pointed at Cole and maybe a couple of inches away from the edge of the bar. The contents, naturally, poured out, drenching the front of Cole's shirt and pants.

Cole glanced at the bartender's face. There was a half smirk on it. He said, "Sorry," and righted the bottle, but he didn't mean the apology and Cole knew it. The spillage had been deliberate, and suddenly a man laughed a few spaces down the bar. The laugh was taken up by others, and the grin on the bartender's face widened.

Cole reached across the bar and got a handful of the bartender's shirt just below his throat. With the considerable strength of which he was capable, he yanked the man toward him.

He put his other hand on the top of the bartender's bald head. With a thump that could be heard all over the noisy room, he slammed the bartender's face down into the spilled whiskey on the bar. And then he rubbed it back and forth several times before releasing it.

The quiet in the saloon was now great enough so that you could have heard a man whisper at the far end of it. All the laughter had stopped, and nobody's face wore a smile.

Cole released the bartender, who straightened up, his face shiny with the spilled whiskey, his nose streaming blood down into his mustache, where it dripped off to run down across his mouth and chin.

The fury in the man's eyes was terrible. Taking one step to his right, he thrust a hand beneath the bar.

Cole knew what he was reaching for. The shotgun. Almost softly, Cole said, "Bartender. Don't do it."

In the act of withdrawing the shotgun, the bartender glanced at Cole. And suddenly he froze. Cole's revolver muzzle was lying on the edge of the bar, pointed straight at the bartender's belly. The hammer was back.

Cole said softly, "Take it out, muzzle pointed away from me. Then lay it on the bar."

Almost as if he were in a trance, the bartender obeyed.

With his left hand, Cole reached out and picked up the gun, a double-barreled ten-gauge. He handed it to Flagg. With his left hand, he picked up his drink, downed it, and laid a quarter on the bar. He put down the glass and took the shotgun away from Flagg. "Finished with your drink?" he asked.

Hastily, Flagg downed his drink and nodded. Cole said, "Then, let's go."

At the door he turned. "You'll find the shotgun outside on the walk." He went on out the door, holstering his revolver as he did. Once outside, he broke the action of the shotgun and ejected the shells. Then he slammed the gun down against the edge of the boardwalk, breaking the stock where it joined the receiver. He tossed both pieces back toward the door of the saloon.

Flagg stared at him with awe mixed with fright. Silently the two crossed the street toward the hotel.

CHAPTER 4

Leaving the saloon, shotgun in one hand, revolver in the other, Cole had kept a pretty close watch on the other occupants of the place. None had seemed inclined to take up the bartender's quarrel. But as he neared the door, he had noticed a small, middle-aged man wearing a dirty apron who caught his glance, held it a moment, then looked quickly away.

As plainly as if he had spoken, Cole understood that the man wanted to talk to him. He also understood that if anybody else had caught the message or if he had in any way acknowledged it, the aproned man's life wouldn't have been worth much.

They reached the hotel and went into the lobby. They crossed it to the dining room and stepped inside. No longer was it crowded. There were half a dozen vacant tables. Probably half a dozen more were still occupied.

Cole and Flagg paused just inside the door. A pretty, and obviously very frightened, waitress crossed to them and stammered, "I am sorry, gentlemen. The dining room is closed."

In a tone that was not unkindly, Cole said, "Tell your boss to come do his own dirty work, young lady. In the meantime, we'll sit down."

He led Flagg to a vacant table that had already been cleaned up. Both men sat down. They waited nearly five minutes, during which time neither the waitress nor her boss appeared. Cole was just pushing his chair back to get up, when a man came from the door leading to the kitchen and approached their table.

From his manner, it was obvious he had heard about the happening in the saloon. He was pale and agitated. He stopped at their table and stammered, "I'm very sorry, gentlemen. The dining room is closed."

Cole said, "Then, open it. And bring a menu. Now."

Cole was normally not an overbearing man. But he had been a law officer for a long time and a soldier before that. He understood the psychology of obtaining the upper hand and keeping it, or the alternative, being a laughing-stock and therefore failing in whatever it was you set out to do. This town was testing him, and if they found him wanting, he might just as well leave and let the marshal's office send somebody else. Or half a dozen, because that was what it would take if he let them run him out of town.

The hotel manager, short and thin and middle-aged, hesitated a moment. Then, with the faintest of shrugs, he retired, returning in a moment with two menus in his hand. He handed one to Flagg and one to Cole, as courteously as if nothing unpleasant had occurred. Cole had the feeling that he had been instructed by someone to refuse them service. Having failed, he was now prepared to treat them like anybody else.

Cole asked, "Tell me something. What's the name of the bartender over at the Drovers Saloon? The bald one with the mustache."

"That's Tod Welch."

"Was he in on the killings down at that Indian camp?" He knew he wasn't going to get an answer but he figured the hotel manager's reaction might tell him what he wanted to know.

It did. The man lost all color and for a moment seemed at a loss for words. Finally he managed to shake his head. "I don't know anything about those killings, sir. I wasn't there and I don't know who was."

Cole nodded, satisfied that Tod Welch had been along. He said, "Send that scared little waitress back. We want to eat."

"Yes sir." The man hurried away, plainly glad to escape.

The waitress came and timidly took their orders. They had been waiting for less than ten minutes when she brought their meal. Cole dug in hungrily. Flagg attacked his food a bit gingerly, meanwhile watching Cole admiringly. "How can you eat like that? After what happened a while ago?"

"That's over. No use letting it spoil my appetite."

Flagg said, "I'll bet, by God, if anybody can get this business straightened out, you can."

"I'm sure going to try." Cole's mouth was full, and he let it go at that.

It had been a long day and Cole was ravenous. He polished off his meal in less than ten minutes and drained his coffee cup. The waitress brought him more, and he took his time over that, while Flagg finished eating.

He didn't mention it to Flagg, but he knew it was going to be a long, long night. The townsmen who had been in on the killings at the Indian camp would try getting rid of the evidence that night. After that, there would be plenty of time for getting rid of him and Flagg and destroying the photographs.

But nothing was going to happen for a while. Not until most of the townspeople had gone to sleep.

Brundage scowled savagely at Cole's back as he strode out of the Drovers Saloon, shotgun in one hand, revolver in the other. Through the window, he watched while Cole ejected the two loads, then smashed the shotgun against the edge of the boardwalk.

He turned his head and looked at Welch. The look on Welch's face was enough to put a cold chill into any man, and Brundage was no exception. Welch was, he decided, the most dangerous man he had ever met. Welch was the one who had turned what started out to be a lark into a mass murder out at the Indian camp. Originally, those participating had meant only to run the Indians off, scatter their horses, and maybe burn their lean-tos or tear them down.

But it had gotten out of hand. Someone had fired a shot. And after the shooting had begun there was only one way it could end: with all the Indians dead.

Brundage turned from the window and walked to the bar. There was still blood on Welch's mustache, even though he was mopping at it with a bar towel. When he saw Brundage he muttered, "I'll kill that dirty son of a bitch! If it's the last thing I ever do, I'll kill that dirty son of a bitch!"

Brundage said, "Then, you better shoot him in the back or you're the one that's going to get killed."

Welch's eyes were grayish green, like the eyes of a cat. He turned them on Brundage and said, "Don't talk to me like that."

Brundage didn't let his glance waver from Welch's virulent one. He said, "And don't you forget who you're talking to." Brundage held the mortgage on Welch's saloon, and it came due in less than ninety days.

Welch looked away, but none of the fury faded from his face. Brundage said, "The thing to do now is decide what should be done. You know who was along that night. Get word to every one of them to meet in the back room of the saloon right away."

"What have you got in mind?"

"Well, those bodies are lying out there just the way you left them. The marshal got Orange to take pictures of them this afternoon. The pictures can be used as evidence in court."

"Then, we got to get the pictures," Welch growled.

"And then he'll take Orange out and get some more. No, the thing that's got to be done first is get rid of the evidence. As soon as the town quiets down, we've got to go out there and clean up the mess. Those bodies have to be hauled away and buried someplace where they'll never be found. The lean-tos and tipis or whatever they were living

in have to be hauled away. The whole place has to be
cleaned up by dragging tree branches back and forth over
it."

"He'll still have the pictures."

"Don't worry about them. Just get everybody together
in the back room right away."

Welch shrugged. "All right." A sly look suddenly came
into his eyes. He said, "You must know you're making
yourself an accessory."

Brundage knew that very well. He also knew that if the
pictures Orange had taken at the Indian camp got spread
all over the front page of the *Rocky Mountain News*, the
future of the town of Coyote Springs would be a shaky
one. People would move away. In a year, it would most
likely be a ghost town, like some of those abandoned min-
ing towns in the mountains west of there.

Welch called to Howie Bracken and told him to look
after the bar. Then he began moving around the room,
stopping here and there to talk to someone, as he often did.
Only, tonight they were the ones who had been along during the slaughter at the Indian camp.

Pat Mosely was the first Welch stopped to talk to. Pat
had previously worked as a cowhand out at the 2 Bar
Ranch. But after the business at the Indian camp, he'd
begun drinking heavily and, finally, Rufus O'Brian, who
owned 2 Bar, fired him. Since then, he'd spent every day
and every night in the Drovers Saloon. Brundage didn't
know where he got the money to pay for his drinks.

Reed Sheridan was the second man Welch stopped to
talk to. Sheridan was the town lawyer, and he ran the ab-

stract company on the side. He was a tall, gangling man, hardly one you would expect to have been along on an expedition like the one that had resulted in so many Indians' deaths. He nodded, got up, and followed Mosely to the back room of the saloon, where there sometimes was a poker game going on.

Arthur Ohlman was the third man Welch talked to. Ohlman got up immediately and went out the front door. Very likely, Brundage thought, he had been sent to fetch those who were not present in the saloon.

Brundage knew who they were: Cliff Tolliver, Pete Olivera, and Marcus Easterling, whose son had been with Keogh's troop at the Little Big Horn in June and had been killed by the Sioux.

Brundage poured himself another drink and downed it. The coming of this marshal and this newspaper reporter constituted the greatest threat his position here in Coyote Springs had ever faced. Somehow it had to be dealt with, no matter what the risk.

Coyote Springs might not be much right now. But Brundage knew, if others did not, that the railroad had surveyed a line through Coyote Springs. And Brundage knew that the coming of the railroad would mean growth and prosperity for the town.

Knowing what he did, he had been quietly buying land on the outskirts of Coyote Springs for months. He had bought every vacant lot in town that was for sale. Everything he owned in the world was here. If the town became a ghost town, he would be wiped out. To avoid that, he was willing to risk making himself an accessory. He was willing to risk almost anything, including getting rid of that marshal, Cole, and the reporter he had brought along with him.

Impatiently he waited for the others to arrive. He started to pour himself another drink, then changed his mind and put the cork into the bottle instead. He would need a clear head, he thought. He didn't want his thinking processes turned fuzzy with alcohol.

CHAPTER 5

When Ohlman came in the door with Sheridan, Olivera, and Marcus Easterling, Brundage got up and followed them to the back room of the saloon. He was the last one in, and he closed the door behind him. He glanced at Welch. "What about Howie?"

Welch said, "Somebody's got to tend bar unless you want me to close the place. Besides, he wasn't actually in on it. He lost his guts and stopped before we actually rode into the camp."

Brundage said, "He could be dangerous. If the marshal gets to him."

Welch snorted, "Hell, Howie hasn't got the guts of a rabbit! You don't need to worry about that."

Brundage shrugged. He looked around at the others. "I suppose you all know that a U.S. marshal and a reporter for the *Rocky Mountain News* arrived in town this afternoon on the stage. The first thing they did was go down to that Indian camp. Then they came back, got Orange, and had him take pictures of it." He paused, feeling his temper and his disgust increase. He said, "It was stupid enough to go down there and do what you did. Leaving it was even stupider, if that's possible. Now something's got to be done or the bunch of you are either going to hang or go to prison. And when the story gets spread over the front page of the *Rocky Mountain News* and picked up by other papers all over the country, this town is through. There may be a lot of people stirred up over the Little Big Horn, but there's just about as many who think that stupid son of a bitch Custer got just what was coming to him."

Marcus Easterling interrupted angrily. "And the men with him too, I suppose?"

"No. I didn't mean that. And I'm sorry, Marcus, about your boy. I'm sorry about the other two hundred and twenty-five that Custer led to their deaths. But the fact remains that those half-starved Arapahoes you men killed had nothing to do with Custer or the Little Big Horn or anything else. They were just traveling and they were unfortunate enough to camp near this town."

Easterling, unmollified, asked, "You're so damn smart, what do you suggest?"

"That place has got to be cleaned up. Tonight. I want a couple of you to get a wagon and team. The rest of you get saddle horses and meet down at the livery stable. We'll all go out to that Indian camp and clean it up. I want at least half a dozen lanterns, six or eight shovels, some ropes so that a couple of you can drag tree branches back and forth over the camp after it's cleaned up, and an ax so that somebody can cut the branches off the trees. They can go out there tomorrow and take all the damn pictures they want but they won't prove a thing in court."

"What about the pictures the marshal's already got?"

"I'll see Orange when we get back. I'll get his plates and destroy them."

"But what about the pictures he made from them? The ones the marshal's got?"

"Let me worry about that."

Ohlman broke in. "No more killing!"

"Nobody said anything about killing anyone."

"Then, how are you going to get the pictures?"

"Don't worry. Just leave it to me."

The men dispersed, leaving the saloon in a group. Welch stopped at the bar to tell Howie to look after things, then followed the others out. He walked home and got his horse out of the stable. He saddled the animal, cursing beneath his breath at the horse's skittishness. Welch had, on some occasions, beaten the horse mercilessly, and the horse was afraid of him. Furthermore, the animal seemed to sense the foul mood he was in.

Welch mounted and rode back toward the center of town. He knew they should have gotten rid of those bodies down at the Indian camp immediately after the shooting, but he hadn't been able to get anyone to go with him and he'd be damned if he was going to do it all by himself. Now he realized that he should have. If he had, they wouldn't have this problem now.

Welch himself felt no regret over the killings at the Indian camp. To him Indians were vermin, to be exterminated whenever and wherever possible. He felt no more regret over killing an Indian child than he would have felt over killing a nest of baby mice.

Now, riding through the darkened streets, he wished he

knew who had snitched to the marshal's office in Denver. In his mind, he went back over those who had participated.

Pat Mosely was the first he considered. Pat had worked pretty steadily, except in winter, as a cowboy before the killings. Afterward he got himself fired from his job and took to spending his days and nights in the saloon, never dropping-down drunk but always feeling the effects sufficiently to make him quarrelsome. Welch didn't know much about human behavior, but he suspected that Mosely's actions lately betrayed a feeling of guilt over what he had helped to do. Still, he couldn't see Mosely contacting the U.S. marshal's office in Denver. Mosely couldn't even write.

Howie Bracken had also gone along, but had dropped out of the bunch before the actual attack. But Howie Bracken didn't have the guts to turn informer. He hadn't even had the guts to stay with the bunch the night of the attack. So he needn't worry about Howie. Howie valued his job too much to give evidence against his boss. Neither could he read or write.

He thought of Reed Sheridan. Next to himself, Reed had seemed to enjoy the whole episode more than anyone. Reed had actually been the leader of the bunch that rode out to the Indian camp that afternoon. But it was Welch himself who had fired the first shot. And after that, everybody had begun shooting, because nobody had known whether the Indians had guns or not. As it turned out, there was one gun in camp, an ancient muzzle-loader that wasn't even loaded when they picked it up and examined it. Welch had taken it home for a souvenir. It was in his closet now.

For several moments, Welch thought about Reed Sheridan. There was something funny about Sheridan, and he wondered what it was. There had been an eagerness in him before they actually reached the Indian camp and something that almost seemed like fear after they did, as if he were going into battle instead of just exterminating a bunch of rats.

Arthur Ohlman was the next one that came to his thoughts. He knew exactly why Ohlman had gone along. Ohlman took a verbal lashing from his wife every day of his life, and Welch knew how bitterly Ohlman hated her. Almost imperceptibly he shrugged. If Ohlman hated the old bitch so much, why didn't he just walk out on her? Or kill her? Or beat her so damned bad she couldn't open her mouth for a month? Those were the things Welch would have done in like circumstances. Yet Ohlman had relieved his frustration by killing out at the Indian camp. Welch had seen him kill the woman in the lean-to, leaving her baby alive and squalling until Welch himself put a bullet into it. Ohlman had emptied his gun into her, and by the time he'd gotten it reloaded, the whole thing had been over with. No, Ohlman wasn't the one who had written the marshal's office. But Ohlman's wife, having found out that he had been involved, might have done so as a means of getting rid of him.

Juan Salgado was next on his mental list. He had first agreed to go when Pat Mosely brought the news of the presence of the Indians. But he'd failed to show up and they had gone without him. Yes, Salgado was a possibility.

So was Cliff Tolliver. He had gone along, but only, apparently, for the purpose of trying to talk them out of molesting the Indians. Finally, a mile before they reached the Indian camp, he had tried to restrain Welch by grabbing the headstall of his horse. Welch had hit him in the mouth, knocking him from the saddle. Tolliver had come on, and had seen what happened from a distance of about a quarter mile. Yes, Tolliver could also have been the one. In fact, he was the most likely of the lot. He was probably the one, since he wasn't along tonight.

Welch cleared Pete Olivera almost instantly in his mind. Olivera had personally shot the old Indian. Nor could Marcus Easterling have been the one. Easterling's son had been with Keogh's troop at the Little Big Horn, and that troop had been wiped out to a man. Easterling had received official notification of his son's death only about a week before the attack on the Indian camp.

All right, then. Salgado was a possibility. But Tolliver was a better choice. Of the eight, he was the most likely to have written the marshal's office. Welch began to think of Tolliver. And he knew what he was going to do. Sometime tonight, if he could, he was going to get Tolliver alone. By the time he was through with him, Tolliver would spill everything he knew.

He arrived at the livery barn. Already the wagon was ready, a team hitched to it. The horses stood silently, patiently, probably picked for their placidity so that they wouldn't act up when they smelled the bodies out at the Indian camp.

Half a dozen lanterns and several shovels were in the back of the wagon. Mosely sat on the driver's seat, waiting for the word to go. Welch said, "Pat, you'd just as well get started. We'll catch up with you."

Mosely slapped the backs of the horses with the reins and they moved on out the door, down the ramp, and into the street, the wagon rumbling along behind. Welch looked around. Easterling was there. So was Reed Sheridan. So were Ohlman and Olivera. Of the eight who had ridden to the Indian camp, only Howie Bracken and Cliff Tolliver were missing, and Howie was working in the saloon, sweeping out, getting it cleaned up for the next day.

Tod Welch said, "All right, let's go. This ain't going to be a pleasant night and there's going to be a lot of puking, but I've got a couple of bottles in my saddlebags if anybody wants a drink."

He led the way down the dark and silent street. Once, he glanced back at the hotel. The lobby was dark, except for the single lamp that burned all night on the clerk's desk. The window of the U.S. marshal's room was dark. The man was probably asleep, Welch thought. After riding a stagecoach all the way from Denver he was probably glad to get into a soft bed and go to sleep.

In silence the five men trotted their horses down the street and across the bridge. Brundage caught up as they made the turn into the two-track road that led to the Indian camp. Welch asked sourly, "What's the matter, didn't you want to take a chance on being seen leaving town with us?"

Brundage said, "No. I didn't want to be seen leaving town at all. Don't forget, I wasn't in on this with you."

Marcus Easterling said, "Nobody meant to kill anybody. We just went down there to run them off. We figured it took a lot of gall for them to camp so close to town after what their Sioux friends did to Custer and his men."

"Then, how did the killing get started?"

Nobody said anything. Brundage persisted, "Well, who fired the first shot?"

Before anybody could answer, Welch said, "There was a gun. One of them sure as hell shot at us."

"What kind of gun?"

"Muzzle-loader," Welch said sullenly.

Brundage looked around at the others. "Is that right?"

Nobody answered. Brundage said sarcastically, "Great! Some poor old Indian shoots at eight men with a one-shot muzzle-loader and misses them. And that's their excuse for murdering everybody in the camp—men, women, and children."

Easterling said angrily, "No use making us sound like butchers! It just got out of hand, that's all. Nobody meant to kill anyone."

Brundage said, "Welch did. He knew when he went down there what was going to happen. Didn't you, Tod?"

Welch growled, "You son of a bitch, you might hold the mortgage on my place, but that don't give you a right to talk to me like that."

"I'll talk to you any damn way I please."

Easterling said, "For Christ's sake, is this bickering getting us anyplace? It's over and done and we all were in on it. I say let's do what we came down here to do. Let's shut up and get rid of the evidence. Brundage has said he'll get the photographs and see to it that Orange's plates are destroyed. Then all we've got to do is sit tight and keep our mouths shut and above all stop bickering with each other over who's to blame. We're all to blame, and that's something we're going to have to live with all the rest of our lives."

Welch growled, "Maybe you're the one that wrote the marshal's office in Denver. You sound like it."

"And maybe, by God, I'm not! Don't use your bullying tactics on me, Welch."

Brundage said disgustedly, "Shut up, all of you. Let's get on down there and get this done."

CHAPTER 6

Frank Cole took his time finishing the last cup of coffee. By now, everyone had left the hotel dining room except Flagg and himself. The pretty young waitress kept eying them nervously, and at last Cole took pity on her and beckoned her for the check. He signed it and put his room number beneath his signature. He left her a tip and then got to his feet. Flagg said, "Next one's on me. I'm on an expense account too."

"All right."

Flagg said, "I'm going to turn in. It's been a damn long day."

"Me too." Cole followed him out of the dining room and up the stairs. He said good night, then went into his room and lighted the lamp. He moved around the room long enough to let himself be seen, then crossed to the window and pulled the shade, satisfied to note that the hidden photographs didn't show. He sat down on the edge of the bed for a few minutes, then got up and blew out the lamp. He raised the shade and peered into the street.

The Drovers Saloon was still going full blast and a number of horses were tied to the rack in front. There were still patrons in the hotel bar as well, and the sound of their talk drifted plainly up to his window. Three horses were tied in front of the hotel.

Frank Cole was tired, but he knew it would be a long time before he'd be able to sleep. This was the night that those who had participated in the massacre out at the Indian camp would try to get rid of the evidence. No later than tomorrow, they'd get Orange's negative plates and destroy them. After that, they'd come after the photographs, and if they didn't find them, would try getting rid of him.

He had no way of knowing how many men had participated in the murders, but he hoped to find out tonight. One, he knew, had gone along only to the edge of the Indian camp in the hope of persuading the others to give it up. He had not participated but had seen everything that occurred. He was the one who had written the U.S. marshal's office in Denver. His name was Cliff Tolliver. He was a cattle buyer, a bachelor who had a room in the hotel and an office across the street from the hotel.

Cole pulled a straight-backed chair over to the window and sat down straddling it, his arms resting on its back, in such a position that he could see the front doors of the Drovers Saloon, across the street. For a while men came and went normally. Finally they stopped coming, and shortly thereafter they began to leave. A few staggered. One seemed to have difficulty telling which of the horses tied before the place was his. Eventually he untied one, mounted, and rode off down the street, and Cole wondered with a wry smile whether he had the right horse or not.

Men kept leaving, one or two at a time. Cole glanced at his watch. It was almost midnight. At last a group of six men left all at once, and he knew that these had to be the ones.

The men scattered. Two went toward the livery stable. The others apparently headed toward their homes.

Cole realized, of course, that it might have been coincidence that six men left simultaneously. The saloon might have been getting ready to close and the remaining patrons told to leave. But he didn't think so.

There wasn't much light in the street, just a little coming from the stars and from a crescent moon. But there was enough to see two of the men turn in at the livery barn.

Satisfied, Cole got up, crammed on his hat, and went out into the hall. He locked his room, pocketed the key, then walked as quietly as he could along the hall and down the back stairs. He went through the kitchen, which was dark and deserted, and out across the yard and into the alley behind the hotel. He paused there for a moment to make sure he was not being observed. Then he headed down the alley toward the livery barn.

Abreast of it, he eased through a weed-grown vacant lot and took up a position in the shadow of a building directly across the street. He could hear voices inside the livery stable. Pretty soon horsemen began to arrive, and not long after that, the wagon drove down the ramp from the livery stable to the street and headed for the bridge at the lower end of town.

The horsemen, four of them, followed in a group after a short delay. Cole waited until both wagon and horsemen had crossed the bridge at the lower end of town. Then he crossed the street.

As he had expected, the livery stable was deserted. He selected a horse from one of the stalls, threw blanket and saddle up, then mounted and rode out into the street. He held the horse to a slow and plodding walk. There was no hurry. It would take the wagon a while to reach the Indian camp, and the horsemen would have no reason to arrive before the wagon did.

In case they had left someone behind to watch for him, Cole halted his horse underneath the bridge and waited patiently for about twenty minutes. No one came and nothing disturbed the silence. Satisfied, Cole rode up from beneath the bridge and took the two-track road leading to the Indian camp. He understood perfectly what they meant to do.

Tonight, Cole hoped to see the face of every man who had participated in the killings at the Indian camp. They had to have lanterns to get anything done. With the pictures he had and the faces and names of the killers, he'd have all he needed. He could make arrests. He could finish this distasteful business and leave Coyote Springs for good.

Except that he knew from experience that it wasn't going to be that easy or that quick. At least six men were ahead of him, their destination the Indian camp. Others might be involved who were not going down to help clean up the place. Arresting two or even three men might be simple enough. Arresting six or more was something else. Unless he had the full co-operation of the sheriff, and he doubted if he was going to get that.

The miles slowly fell behind. Once, he stopped and waited a full five minutes after catching the faint sound of a man's voice from ahead. Finally he went on and a few minutes later brought several flickering lanterns into sight.

He immediately dismounted, led his horse into the trees that bordered the creek, and tied him there. On foot, he returned, working himself ever closer to the lanterns and to the men working by their light.

Mosely had driven the wagon to the site of the Indian camp. The horses, placid though they were, hadn't liked the smell and had had to be forced by laying the whip across their backs. Somewhere short of the first body, Mosely had stopped the team. Easterling, after tying his horse to a tree, had lighted a lantern. He'd walked ahead, beckoning Mosely to follow him.

The first body was that of the ten- or eleven-year-old boy. Easterling stared down, suddenly and unexpectedly remembering when his own boy, James, the one killed at the Little Big Horn in June, had been this age. He'd had his doubts about this business, the first beginning at the time they charged into this little Indian camp firing at everything that moved. He'd had more doubts since. But this was the first time he'd been here since the actual killing had taken place, nearly a month before.

The smell of the body struck him, and he saw the way both abdominal cavity and face had been eaten away by vultures. His stomach suddenly contracted and, despite his determination not to let it happen, he bent double and vomited the contents of his stomach on the ground.

Mosely seemed to be little better off. His face, in the lantern light, was green. Perhaps as angry at himself as at Easterling, he said, "Come on, for Christ's sake! Give me a hand to throw him in the wagon."

His stomach empty, Easterling complied. But as he lifted the boy's legs, the dry heaves took him. He and Mosely dropped the body into the wagon bed and moved on to the lean-to, where the body of the woman and her baby lay.

Mosely drove. Easterling walked behind. How could he have participated in such a thing? Easterling asked himself desperately. Well, he hadn't intended to. When Pat Mosely had brought the news to town that a bunch of Indians were camped out there, the intention had been only to ride out and run them off. Drive them away. Scatter their horses and burn their tipis or whatever it was they were living in.

The whites had all had guns, of course. Easterling remembered that as they rode out toward the Indian camp, he had been thinking of his son, James, and remembering the last time he had seen his boy, decked out in his trooper's uniform, proud of himself and the way he looked, proud too that he would be serving under Colonel Custer, who had been a general during the war.

Easterling reminded himself that he had personally not fired his gun except into the air. It was small consolation, but it helped. He had not, himself, killed any of these pitifully poor Indians.

Nor could he definitely say who had. Everything had been too confused. Maybe no shots would have been fired at all if one of the Indians, in possession of an ancient muzzle-loader, hadn't brandished it.

Mosely held the lantern while Easterling looked into the lean-to where the dead Indian woman and her baby lay. There, at least, the vultures had not torn the bodies, but they were badly bloated and decomposed. Not enough, though, to hide the large brown stains from the blood that had soaked the woman's clothes. Nor to hide the blood on the baby's chest from the single bullet that had taken its life.

Someone, thought Easterling with a shock, had literally emptied his gun into the helpless woman in the lean-to. Who? Which one of the men who had been along that day was capable of that kind of savagery?

One by one, he went over them in his mind, as he watched Mosely lift the baby's body and lay it in the wagon bed. Mosely? No. He was nearly as sickened right now as Easterling was himself.

Then a name came to him, and he knew that Tod Welch must have murdered this woman and her child. Tod Welch was probably the only one of them capable of this kind of savagery, this kind of sadistic cruelty.

Mosely said impatiently, "Come on, come on! I don't want to be here all night. I don't like this any better than you do."

Easterling lifted the woman's shoulders, startled at how little she weighed. He helped Mosely lift her body over the side of the wagon. Almost gently, despite the nausea troubling them both, they laid her down.

Down toward the creek, Easterling could hear the ring of axes as a couple of the men cut branches for dragging across the area. Welch rode to the wagon, saying, "Come on, come on! We haven't got all night."

Easterling stopped following the wagon toward the next body. He looked up at Welch. "It was you, wasn't it? You're the one who started it and you're the one who killed most of them."

"What the hell are you talking about? We all were in on it. Now, get busy and finish loading them up. I'll get a couple of other men to tear their lean-tos down."

Easterling balked. He said, "You finish loading them. I want to see if you puke the way I did."

Welch dismounted. Leading his horse, he followed the wagon. He helped Mosely lift the next body, but instead of laying it gently in the wagon, he tossed it in like so much dead meat.

Easterling watched him with disgust until he realized he had no right to feel disgust for anyone. Not for Welch, not for anyone who had been present here the afternoon those killings had all taken place.

Each one of them was as guilty as the next. In the eyes of the law, it didn't matter who had killed which Indian or how many bullets had been used to kill each one. Age or sex didn't matter either. Every man who had ridden into this Indian camp was as guilty as the next. He was as guilty as Welch, and if they came to trial, he would pay the same penalty.

What would James think of him now? Easterling wondered. James had worn the uniform of his country with pride. He had fought bravely and well, following the orders of his commanding officer, the way a soldier is supposed to do.

And to avenge his death, his father had ridden out here with a sadistic butcher and participated in the murder of nearly a dozen poor, half-starved, itinerant Indians who didn't even belong to the same tribe that had annihilated Custer's command.

Well, this job had to be done unless he wanted to hang

or spend the rest of his life in prison. He turned away from the wagon, went back to the lean-to in which the woman and her baby had been killed, and began, almost frantically, to tear it down, as if by obliterating this physical evidence he could erase from his mind the way the woman had looked with her bloated and decomposed baby lying at her side.

Never, as long as he lived, would the sights he had seen this night fade from his mind. For an instant he had the compulsion to go to the U.S. marshal and confess. For an instant he wanted to take his punishment, serve his penance, whatever it might be.

Then he thought of his wife. She had lost her son, and still wept in the night for him. If he was hanged or if he went to prison his wife would die. Nor would his punishment, even if it eased his own guilt, bring any of the dead Indians back to life.

No. He had better go along with the others, covering up the crime as best they could. Maybe, eventually, time would ease the pain in his mind and heart. He could only pray it would.

Only, how could a man pray after he has done something as terrible as all of them had done here in this Indian camp? Easterling had no answer to give himself for that.

CHAPTER 7

Frank Cole watched from the darkness as the men loaded the bodies of the dead Indians into the wagon. He saw several of them double and vomit on the ground.

Five lanterns had been lighted in all. By the lantern light, he was able to clearly see the face of each of the seven men present at the scene.

He did not yet, of course, know all their names. He would learn them later. But Cole had an infallible memory for faces, and he knew he would forget none of these.

He did recognize Tod Welch, the bartender at the Drovers Saloon, with whom he'd had the argument earlier. Welch seemed to be the only one who felt no revulsion for what he was doing tonight.

He also recognized Carl Brundage and noticed that he took no part in the loading of bodies or tearing down the pitiful shelters the Indians had built. But Brundage was obviously in charge and giving most of the orders, orders that were obeyed, however sullenly, even by Tod Welch.

The bodies finally were loaded. The shaky lean-tos and

shelters were demolished and loaded into the wagon on top
of them. Two men tied ropes to sizable tree branches that
had been cut and began dragging them back and forth
across the place where the camp had been. As the wagon
drove away, with three horsemen following, Cole edged
back into the trees that lined the stream and found his
horse.

Both men dragging tree branches around the Indian
camp had lanterns. The others had been extinguished and
loaded into the wagon. So Cole had to follow it by sound.

It was going to be necessary later that he be able to find
the site of the burial. The evidence would be needed when
the killers were brought to trial. He therefore took bearings on the stars, took other bearings on whatever land-
marks were visible, and even lighted a match in a place
where a knoll concealed him from the wagon, to consult
his watch.

The crescent moon traveled across the sky. The men
driving the wagon and those following it were a glum lot,
so he wasn't able to follow by the sound of voices. And the
wagon wheels made very little sound in the soft prairie
grass. Fortunately, however, one of the axles needed grease
and squeaked intermittently.

Cole tried to stay as far behind as possible, but he didn't
dare get so far back that his ears lost the sound of the
squeaking wheel. He could have come out here tomorrow,
he thought, and followed the wagon tracks to the place
where the bodies were buried, but it was better to find the
location now. Tomorrow, in daylight, he would almost
certainly be followed, and might even be attacked or shot.
And even if he did find the burial place, those guilty of the

killings would know it and would move the bodies the night following.

Eventually, the wagon and those following it reached a place Brundage had apparently decided would be safe. It was at the foot of a bluff. The wagon halted and the lanterns were again lighted. Cole stopped his horse about three hundred yards away, making sure he was neither upwind nor downwind from the wagon horses and the three saddle animals. He didn't want his horse giving him away.

There was a clanking as shovels were taken from the wagon bed. Two of the men began digging a single grave in the rocky ground. They worked steadily and, after about fifteen minutes, were relieved by two of the other men.

Cole positioned himself behind his horse, lighted a match, and swiftly glanced at his watch. It had taken the wagon exactly an hour and seventeen minutes to reach this spot. The direction had been almost exactly west. And there couldn't be more than one bluff like this one for miles.

Now he put his mind to locating the exact position of the grave. That wasn't hard. There was a huge boulder, higher than a man, less than a dozen yards from the grave, a boulder that apparently had tumbled down off the rim at some time in ages past.

He could come directly to this place again. He had no doubt of that.

Once more, the diggers were relieved. By the lantern light, Cole could see that they now were down about five feet. Suddenly Brundage said, "All right, that's deep enough. Let's throw 'em in and get the hell out of here."

The wagon was driven close to the grave. One by one, the bodies were dumped into it, each with a thud that Cole could faintly hear even three hundred yards away. Afterward, the dismantled lean-tos were throw in too, and after that the earth was shoveled in.

A large mound of it was left. Cole heard Welch growl, "You're so goddam smart. What are we going to do with that?"

"Why do you think I had you put the grave at the foot of this slope? Take a couple of men with shovels and go about halfway up that slope. There's plenty of rocks up there that can be dislodged, and as they come down they'll bring a landslide along with them."

If Welch replied to that, Cole didn't hear what he said. He heard the sounds of two or three men scrambling up the slope. The wagon rolled into motion, and the others, leading horses and still carrying lighted lanterns, followed it. It halted several hundred yards away.

Cole already knew exactly what he needed to know. But still he waited curiously, wanting to see how successful this landslide business was going to be. The big rock gave him an indestructible landmark no matter how much rubble came down on top of the grave.

After a few minutes he heard a large rock begin its bounding journey to the level plain. True to Brundage's expectations it knocked loose other rocks, which in turn loosened other, smaller rocks and earth. Dust rose in a cloud.

Knowing that the slide had effectively concealed the grave and the loose dirt left over from it, Cole mounted his horse and headed, at a walk, back toward town. Only when he was a quarter mile away did he touch heels to the horse's sides and urge him to a lope. Some of the men behind him might also hurry back toward town. He wanted to arrive before they did, put the horse away, and reach his hotel room before they arrived in town.

It took much less time returning than it had coming. He arrived in town, took the horse directly to the stable, and unsaddled him. But instead of returning him to the stall, he led him to the corral out back and turned him loose so that no one would notice he had been used. Then, cutting through the vacant lot and crossing the street quickly, he headed for the back door of the hotel.

There was a light in the kitchen, and he cursed softly beneath his breath. The cook probably came very early to get things started for breakfast. He circled the hotel, cutting between it and the building next to it, and, looking down the street, saw several horsemen coming up the street from the bridge, dim shapes in the nearly complete lack of light.

Walking as softly as he could, he climbed the steps to the hotel veranda and peered into the lobby.

It was lighted by only one lamp, that one sitting on the clerk's desk. By its faint light he could see the clerk sitting in a straight-backed chair tilted back against the wall. The clerk's chin was on his chest and his eyes appeared to be closed.

Cole didn't know whether he was asleep or not. In any event, he couldn't stay out there, because of the horsemen coming up the street, and he was damned if he was going to risk having to hide until morning if the horsemen happened to wake the clerk.

Quietly he walked into the lobby, across it, and up the steps. Halfway up he turned his head and glanced back at the clerk. The man hadn't changed position. Apparently he was sound asleep.

Cole reached the head of the stairs. It was important to him that the men he had followed and observed tonight didn't know he had. He didn't want them moving the bodies of the Indians again, to a place where he wouldn't be able to find them, and he couldn't watch seven men forever all by himself.

Silently he unlocked his room, stepped inside, and closed the door behind him. He relocked it and pocketed the key.

All of a sudden, now, weariness struck him. He'd ridden that damned stagecoach from seven this morning until its arrival here in Coyote Springs. He'd been up almost the whole damned night. He couldn't see the face of his watch and he didn't want to risk lighting a match or a lamp, but he was willing to bet it was nearly dawn.

At least, he thought, the seven conspirators were nearly as tired as he. He sat down on the edge of the bed, pulled off his boots, laid his hat and gun on a chair beside the bed, and closed his eyes. He was almost instantly asleep.

Tod Welch, assigned to drive the wagon back to town and accompanied by Marcus Easterling, drove in sour silence, forcing the horses to trot even though he had to periodically lay the whip across their backs to force them to maintain that gait.

Once he growled, "What time is it?"

Easterling took out his gold hunting-case watch and struck a match so that he could see the face. He said, "Two forty-five."

Welch growled, "It's goin' to be light before we get this damned rig back to town."

"We can come in by that old back road. We can get to the stable from the rear. Besides, it won't be much later than five-thirty or six, will it?"

"How the hell do I know? I didn't keep track of our driving time."

Both men lapsed into silence. Welch was thinking about the episode with Cole that afternoon. He had spilled the whiskey deliberately and Cole had known it was deliberate. So had everybody else.

Welch felt his face getting warm. He was the one who had come out of that incident looking bad. Cole had come out looking tough and competent, a man dangerous to cross. Welch would have blasted him with the shotgun if he'd been able to get his hands on it. Only, once more Cole had been too quick for him.

Well, that was going to change. Brundage might think he was in charge of this whole thing, but he wasn't. Welch was going to kill Cole. One way or another, he didn't care. Nobody was going to rub his face in spilled whiskey and get away with it. Nobody was going to take his shotgun, deliberately smash it to pieces, and then contemptuously throw the pieces away.

It was true that nobody had laughed. But Welch knew he had lost a lot of stature. The only way he was going to regain it was by killing Cole.

He began to think again of that raid on the Indian village. He remembered Pat Mosely coming into the saloon yelling that there was a bunch of dirty Indians camped down on the creek. He'd yelled, "Let's go down and run 'em off! Let's burn their stuff and chase 'em to hell out of here. First thing you know, they'll be killin' somebody's beef. Or maybe killin' people if they happen to get in the way."

It hadn't taken long for the enthusiasm for the raid to build up inside the saloon. Welch rarely closed his place in the middle of the day, but he'd closed it that day. He wouldn't have missed that raid for anything.

The big mistake they'd made, Welch realized now, was that they hadn't gone out and buried those Indians and gotten rid of their shelters right away. The next day. The trouble had been that all who had taken part in the slaughter had been ashamed of what they'd done. Except for himself, they'd all been shocked at the way the thing had gotten out of hand. Except for himself, they'd all really only intended to run the Indians off. But when the shooting had started, all of them had taken part—Except for Tolliver, who had hung back and had never reached the Indian camp at all. And except for Howie Bracken, who bolted when the first shot was fired and joined Tolliver.

Well, it was over now. Brundage had said he would take care of Orange's negative plates. He'd promised to get the prints from Cole.

Welch smiled grimly to himself. Doing that was going to be a lot tougher than just saying it. Frank Cole was tough. The only way of getting rid of him might be shooting him in the back. And that was a job for which he'd gladly volunteer.

CHAPTER 8

Frank Cole had expected no trouble this night, and he got none. He'd figured the perpetrators of the massacre at the Indian camp would be too tired to bother him, and he had been right.

He awoke at dawn as he always did. Gray lightened the horizon in the east, rapidly changing to the faintest of pinks, which grew stronger and brighter with every passing moment.

Cole supposed he hadn't slept much more than an hour and a half, but he knew that no matter how he tried, he would sleep no more. He ought to try to nap a while this afternoon, he thought. If he didn't, he was going to be so damned tired tonight that they could ransack his room without even waking him.

He got off the bed, washed his face in cold water, and shaved. He dug a wrinkled but clean white shirt out of his carpetbag, pinned the marshal's badge to the pocket, then put on his vest. He buckled his gun and cartridge belt around his waist, ran a comb through his hair, and put on his hat.

He glanced at himself in the mirror before he turned toward the door. His was an angular, bony face, with prominent cheekbones, a jutting chin, a rounded and jutting forehead. He wore a mustache that was wide and sweeping. It seemed to be a part of him, so much a part of him that most men who knew him could not imagine what he would have looked like without it.

His mouth was also wide, neither grim nor humorous, and certainly not soft. But he had a sense of humor, enjoyed the company of companionable other men and liked both women and children, sometimes regretting that he had neither wife nor children of his own. His encounters with women had invariably been with prostitutes or saloon girls except for the first, when he had been initiated into the mysteries of sex at age twelve by a sixteen-year-old hired girl who helped his mother on the farm. He still, when the strong smell of hay reached his nostrils, remembered that encounter, which had scared him at the time but only amused him now because of its mutual clumsiness.

The clerk, who had been sleeping when he came in a while ago, was now awake.

Cole nodded at him and headed for the back door. He went out behind the hotel, where there was a small, barren yard turned white by soapsuds thrown out the kitchen door by the help. There was a pump and washstand near the door, and out at the alley were two outhouses, one labeled MEN, the other, WOMEN. Cole met Flagg coming out and spoke to him. Flagg asked, "Sleep well?" and Cole shrugged noncommittally.

When he emerged from the outhouse, Flagg was at the washstand. Cole washed his hands, then went back through the hotel lobby to the street. He could hear the sounds of dishes rattling from the direction of the dining room, but after his hostile reception there last evening, had no desire to eat in the hotel again if he could find another place.

By the time he reached the street, the sun was poking above the horizon, turning the golden cottonwoods an even more brilliant yellow that cast a warm glow over the entire town.

The air was cool and had the winy bite peculiar to the atmosphere in fall. Cole took a couple of deep breaths and headed down the street.

Less than a block below the hotel there was a restaurant so small that he had not even noticed it the day before. He tried the door, found it unlocked, and went inside. No one was in the place, but he smelled coffee. There was a counter with five stools, and there were two tables, each with four chairs. He sat at the counter, and a moment later a woman came from the door that led to the kitchen.

She appeared to be at least five years younger than Cole. As she came through the door her expression was one of smiling welcome that changed subtly when she saw who he was. The change told him she knew him—knew his job and why he was there. But despite her coolness there was something about her that attracted him to her instantly. He smiled and said, "Good morning, ma'am. Am I too early for breakfast?"

She shook her head. Her voice, when it came, was pleasant: a bit husky but warm and soft. "Of course not. Would you like some coffee first?"

"Yes ma'am." He watched her turn, watched her go back through the door into the kitchen, admiring the way she moved, admiring too the straightness of her back and the full roundness of her hips.

She was back in a moment, a steaming cup of coffee in her hand. She placed it in front of him, then brought a cream pitcher and a sugar bowl. She asked, "What would you like to eat?"

Cole sipped the coffee. Instead of answering, he asked, "You know who I am?"

She nodded but did not smile. "Strangers are rare in Coyote Springs."

He said, "My name's Frank Cole. What's yours?"

His directness seemed to both confuse and irritate her. Yet, because there was nothing inherently offensive about his question, she answered it. "I'm Nora McKissick. Mrs. Nora McKissick."

"You have a husband, then?"

Now her face colored slightly with resentment at his inquisitiveness. "No. I am a widow."

Cole realized with some surprise that he liked this woman and wanted to know her well. She started to speak, probably to repeat her question regarding what he wanted to eat, but he interrupted her. "If you know who I am, then you know why I'm here."

"Of course."

"And you don't like me because of what I have to do?"

Her expression was now openly exasperated. "Mr. Cole, you came in here for breakfast. I have given you coffee. Now, if you will tell me what you want to eat, I'll fix it for you."

But Cole would not give up so easily. "Why?"

"Why what?"

"Why don't you like me? You're not the kind of woman who would condone the murder of innocent people, even if they were Indians."

"How do you know what kind of woman I am?" Her eyes met his directly, and he realized that they were a very lovely shade of gray. He said, "I guess I don't, except that people pretty much look like what they are inside."

She hesitated, undecided between exploding angrily and answering. She decided on the latter and said, "I don't condone what happened out there, but I had a brother with Custer at the Little Big Horn. He was only seventeen."

"I'm sorry. I had no right to question you." He was genuinely regretful, and sorry he had reminded her of something as painful as her brother's death. He said, "I'll have some bacon and eggs if you have them."

She nodded, giving him a faint smile now, as if trying to say that, after four months, the pain of her loss had eased. She turned and went back into the kitchen. Cole sipped his coffee, more stirred by this woman than he could ever recall being stirred before. She had suddenly made him realize how empty his life actually was. He caught himself wondering what it would be like to return to such a woman every night for the rest of his life.

He could smell bacon cooking now and could hear the grease splattering. Nora McKissick stuck her head through the door and asked, "Need more coffee yet?"

His cup was still half full but he nodded anyway just to get her back out where he could look at her. She brought the pot and filled his cup. Cole groped for something he could say that would hold her there, but could think of nothing. She returned to the kitchen.

He continued to sip the coffee. He smelled biscuits, and a little later she brought his breakfast, a large platter with bacon, three eggs, biscuits, butter, and strawberry jam. Cole regarded it appreciatively.

Nora started to return to the kitchen but Cole said, "Stay and talk to me."

Hands on hips, she studied him, half amused, half exasperated. "You're a very direct man, Mr. Cole."

"Frank. My friends call me Frank, and I think you and I are going to be friends."

Suddenly she laughed, and he liked the sound of her laugh as much as he liked the sound of her voice. He began to eat, grinning a little as he did. She got a stool from the kitchen, brought it in behind the counter, and sat down on it.

He guessed the conversation had gone far enough along this tack, so he asked, "Tell me about your brother. Whose troop was he in?"

"Captain Keogh's troop. With Mrs. Easterling's boy."

"How long had he been in?"

"Less than six months. They sent him to Fort Abraham Lincoln right away and assigned him to the Seventh Cavalry. He was so excited to be serving under such a famous general. And he was pleased to be in the same troop with James Easterling."

"What do you think of Custer?"

She shook her head. "I don't know what to think. There are so many things in the newspapers. Some of the accounts make him out to be a hero. There are others, suggesting that he disobeyed his orders, that he was in trouble with his superiors and was willing to risk everything, including his men, in order to achieve a spectacular victory. What do *you* think of him?"

Cole decided this was not the best time for airing his own views. He temporized. "I think he ought to have known better than to attack several thousand Indians with no more men than he had."

She apparently didn't want to pursue the subject any further, either. She got up, brought the pot, and again refilled his coffee cup. By now, hungry as he had been, he had nearly finished his breakfast.

Still direct and blunt, he said, "There are a couple of questions I'd like to ask."

Her expression was questioning.

"Is anybody courting you?"

Her face flamed suddenly with embarrassment. A little numbly, she shook her head.

Cole said, "Then, there must be a lot of fools living in this town. Do you mind if I come and see you again?"

Now very flustered, she began gathering up his dishes. Almost lamely she said, "The restaurant is open from seven in the morning until seven at night."

"That's not what I meant."

Her eyes rose and met his squarely. "You're not staying here. You've only come to do a job. When it's finished, you will leave."

"Nothing's forever and I'm not trifling. I want to see you again."

She didn't seem to know how to reply, and there was

something in her eyes that was almost like fright. But at last she nodded wordlessly.

Cole gave her a warm, reassuring smile. He laid half a dollar on the counter, then turned and went out the door, a little surprised, himself, at the direct way he had talked with her.

Brundage, who opened his store at seven, saw Cole go into Nora McKissick's restaurant, down the street. Immediately, he turned away from the still-locked door of his store and hurried instead up the street to the house of Lucas Orange. He banged on the door, which had been locked for the night, and Orange opened it. Brundage wasted no time. "I want those plates."

"I can't . . . what if that marshal—?"

Brundage uttered a disgusted obscenity. "The plates. Now!"

Orange hadn't what it took to face Brundage down. He shrugged and held the door for Brundage to come in. He went right to the plates, picked them up, and handed them to Brundage, who asked, "Is this all of them?"

Orange nodded.

Brundage said, "You'd better not be lying to me."

"Why would I lie? Besides, the plates are no good any more. He's got the prints."

Brundage suddenly raised the heavy stack of glass negatives over his head. He threw them onto the floor with all the force of which he was capable. They smashed, but, still not satisfied, he stirred them with his toe to make sure they were all broken. Then he said, "Sweep them up and dump them in the ashpit." He fished in his pocket and came up with a five-dollar gold piece, which he handed to Orange. "They've been misplaced, or routinely destroyed, or coated again, or whatever story you want to tell. Understand?"

Orange nodded, already heading for the corner and the broom. Brundage turned and went outside.

So far so good. The evidence and the plates were gone. Remaining were only the prints, the marshal, and that rabbit of a reporter from the *Rocky Mountain News*.

CHAPTER 9

From the window of his store, Brundage kept an eye on the Drovers Saloon, down the street. Howie Bracken invariably came at eight and opened up. He swept out, emptied the spittoons, washed whatever glasses hadn't been washed the night before, and generally got the place ready for another day of business. Tod Welch didn't usually come until nine, which was the hour he opened for business. Nine was early for most people, but if there were cowhands in town with hangovers, it wasn't nearly early enough, for them at least.

Brundage absent-mindedly waited on a couple of the ladies of the town and later couldn't even have said who they were. At eight, he saw Howie Bracken come shuffling up the street from the direction of his one-room shack down at the edge of the creek. Howie unlocked the doors, fastened them back, then went inside and released the swinging doors.

Brundage went out without bothering to lock his door.

He walked along the street and crossed to the Drovers Saloon. He pushed the doors open.

Howie had a spittoon in each hand and was carrying them out back to dump them in the outhouse. Brundage said, "Never mind those right now. There's something I want you to do."

Howie paused. He was a thin little man of about forty-five. So far as Brundage knew, he had never held any job but cleaning up around a saloon and filling in as bartender during a rush. He could clean and he could pour whiskey and he could draw beer as well as anyone. Brundage knew he could neither read nor write, but he was able to support himself and he seemed happy enough. Brundage said, "Lock the saloon and go round up all the men who were in on that thing out at the Indian camp. Tell them to meet in the back room of my store at nine. Tell them to come in the back door."

Howie nodded, put down the spittoons, and wiped his hands on the dirty apron he wore. Brundage went out and Howie followed, locking the saloon doors behind him. Brundage returned to his store and Howie set off in the direction of Arthur Ohlman's barbershop.

Ina Blair arrived at ten minutes of nine exactly, just as she always did. Ina worked in the store. She was never either a minute early or a minute late. It was a point of pride with her. Brundage told her he'd be busy in the back room for a while and not to disturb him. Then he went back to the storeroom at the rear of the building and dropped the bar into place so the door couldn't be opened unexpectedly.

The wall between storeroom and store was solid stone,

the storeroom having been added on after the building had been built. Voices wouldn't carry through.

Howie Bracken was the first to arrive. He looked scared. He came in and sat down nervously on a nail keg. He stared steadily at the floor between his knees. Brundage had not, of course, been out at the Indian camp at the time of the shooting. But he'd heard what had happened often enough, from one or another of the participants. He knew that Howie Bracken had ridden only as far as the edge of the camp. At the first shot, he had whirled his horse and bolted. But Welch had threatened him. He had convinced him that he was as guilty as any of those who had actually done the killing. He had also told him he would lose his job if he ever talked to anyone about that day.

Pat Mosely came in next, a little unsteady and reeking of whiskey. Reed Sheridan came next, followed by Arthur Ohlman. Welch came a little after nine o'clock. All the men filed in, found themselves places to sit, and waited.

The others didn't come. Cliff Tolliver's absence didn't surprise Brundage very much. Marcus Easterling's did. And Brundage had expected Pete Olivera to show.

He looked at Howie Bracken. "You see Tolliver and Easterling and Olivera?"

Bracken looked up and nodded. "Yes sir."

Brundage looked at Welch. "Maybe you'd better go see them. Convince them they'd better come. If we don't hang together, we may hang separately. Tell them that. Tell them too that it don't make a damn bit of difference who shot who. Everybody that was out there is equally guilty and I'm an accessory."

Tod Welch got up, scowling. He went out. He walked

swiftly up the alley toward the upper end of town, wanting to see Easterling first.

He knocked at the Easterling back door. Mrs. Easterling
answered it. She wasn't weeping now, but her eyes were
red. Not surprising, Welch supposed. She'd lost her son at
the Little Big Horn. Now this marshal was in town, and if
he did what he'd been sent to do, she might lose her husband too. He said, "Is Marcus here, Mrs. Easterling?"

"He's here, but he's not going with you. He's through
with what happened at that Indian camp. It's over with."

"Not quite, Mrs. Easterling." Welch's words in themselves were respectful enough but his tone was not. There
was an edge of threat in it. He said, "You know about that
marshal and reporter that are in town."

"But you all went out last night. . . ." A touch of anger
came to her voice. "Do you realize how sick he was when
he came home last night?"

"All of us were sick. Go tell him to come on out."

"No."

Welch's face turned red. He said in a softly even tone,
"Damn you, woman, do what I tell you to! Or I'll come in
and drag him out of there myself!"

Easterling came to the kitchen door and crossed the
porch. "That won't be necessary. I'm coming. But don't
you ever talk to my wife like that again!"

Welch gave him a look that contained nothing but con-
tempt. He knew Easterling had been in the kitchen all the
time, listening. He walked down the alley toward town,
with Easterling keeping pace half a step behind. Where he
had to turn off to go to Tolliver's office, he stopped Easterling. He said, "I'm not going to chase you all over town
every time you're wanted. You understand?"

Easterling said, "To hell with you."

Welch hit him in the mouth. Easterling staggered backward from the force of the blow and crashed against a
rickety fence. He sat there staring up at Welch with disbelief, blood running from his mouth and smashed lips.
Welch said, "Remember, when you're sent for, you come.
You're in this just as deep as anyone. If one of us hangs,
we're all going to hang." He turned and walked away. Easterling got up, one hand holding a white handkerchief to
his mouth, the other trying, rather ineffectually, to brush
the alley dirt from his clothes. Finally he walked unsteadily down the alley toward Brundage's store.

Tod Welch cut through a vacant lot and climbed the
outside wooden stairs to Tolliver's office, over the bank,
diagonally across the intersection from the hotel.

Tolliver was sitting at his desk, which was piled high
with papers. Welch said, "Howie told you there was a
meeting down in the back room of Brundage's store, didn't
he?"

"He told me. But I'm not coming."

Welch was standing across the desk from him. Suddenly
he seized the edge of the desk and heaved it over on top of
Tolliver, whose swivel chair overturned, allowing the edge
of the desk to come down across his legs. He let out a howl
of pain.

Welch said, "Get up and come on. I'm not going to fool
with you, Tolliver. Maybe you didn't kill anybody, but
you were there, and that makes you just as guilty as the
rest of us."

Tolliver struggled out from underneath the desk. For an
instant there was defiance in his face, but then Welch
said, "I'm looking at a murder charge and so are all the rest

of us. Do you think one more killing will make it any worse?"

Tolliver stared dumbly at him. Finally he nodded his head. "All right. I'll come."

Welch said, "Right away." He went out and down the stairs, leaving Tolliver staring at the mess of papers scattered on his floor.

Olivera lived with his wife and five children in a run-down two-story house half a block from the creek. He was a carpenter and today was repairing a fence behind his house. Welch said, "You were sent for. Why the hell didn't you come?"

"Because it's stupid, that's why. We all get together and that U.S. marshal sees us and it's just like giving him a list of names. Besides, they were only a bunch of dirty Indians. No damn jury in the country is going to convict us of killing them."

Welch said, "You come. You come right now. Dirty Indians or not, if that marshal gets enough evidence, he's going to throw us all in jail and see that we go to trial."

He was looking at Olivera's kids, playing in the yard. He looked beyond them at the run-down house. He said, "That place looks like a firetrap."

Olivera understood. He put down his hammer, took off his nail apron, and hung it on the fence. He said, "All right. I'll be right there. Just give me time to tell my wife."

Welch nodded. He turned and headed back toward Brundage's store. A block short of it, he saw Easterling hurrying up the alley toward home.

He immediately broke into a run. Easterling turned the corner out of the alley with Welch only a dozen yards behind. Easterling was running now, but it didn't do him any good. Welch caught him as he turned into the next alley and brought him down behind a huge, two-story stable standing behind the widow Wallace's two-story house.

Easterling started to shout, so Welch smashed his fist into Easterling's mouth. Easterling tried to get away, crawling, and made it into the stable. His hands seized a singletree hanging from a nail, and he swung around, obviously intending to use the singletree as a club or at least threaten Welch with it.

Welch stopped, and spread his hands in a peaceful gesture. "All right. All right. Stay out of it if it's that important to you. Maybe you're right anyway. Maybe losin' your boy and all—" He turned away.

Easterling relaxed. He dropped the singletree. He headed for the door.

This was what Welch had been waiting for. Whirling, he shouldered Easterling back with such force that the man fell. Welch stooped and grabbed the singletree. Swinging it viciously as Easterling came to hands and knees, he struck the man solidly on the side of the head with enough force to crush Easterling's skull.

He didn't need a second look to know that Easterling was dead. Dropping the singletree, he went to the door and peered outside. The alley was deserted.

He stepped out, closing the door behind him. He walked down the alley to the street, glancing both up and down before he stepped out into it. When Easterling's body was found, he didn't want anyone saying he had seen him in the neighborhood.

Satisfied that the street was deserted, he walked along it

at a normal rate of speed to the alley that ran behind the Brundage store. When he arrived, both Tolliver and Olivera were already there.

Brundage asked, "Didn't you see Easterling?"

Welch nodded. "Sure. I went to his house for him. He said he was coming down."

Brundage shrugged. "Well, we can't wait all day. We've got to decide what we're going to do."

CHAPTER 10

At ten o'clock, Dave Thorne, sheriff of Maxwell County, rode into Coyote Springs. He was dead tired, having ridden all night, and all he wanted to do was to go home and fall into bed. He had been serving an eviction paper for the bank, clear over at the far end of the county, sixty miles away, and he had been gone three days.

Instead of being allowed to go straight home and go to bed, however, he was met in front of his office a block down the street from the Colorado Hotel by a gang of kids and a hysterical widow Wallace, all screaming at him that Mr. Easterling was lying in the widow's stable with his head smashed in.

It looked like half the people in town were already running or walking in the direction of the widow Wallace's house. Cursing sourly to himself, Thorne kicked his weary horse in the ribs, forcing him to trot, and rode up the street after the crowd.

They were clustered three deep in front of the alley

door to Mrs. Wallace's stable. Thorne dismounted and shoved his way through.

Victor Rensling, the veterinarian, was kneeling beside the body. He glanced up as Thorne came in. He shook his head. "Dead. Skull crushed. Died instantly."

Thorne looked around. He saw the singletree lying on the manure-littered dirt floor. "Think that did it?"

Rensling nodded. "Could have." He was a tall and gangling man. He stood up, shoulders stooped, hair untidy and uncut. He wore a Vandyke beard that needed trimming, and his necktie had gravy spots on it. You could tell he was a bachelor just by looking at him.

Thorne turned his head toward the curious crowd at the door. "Will somebody go after Norman Reeves? Tell him to bring the hearse."

Somebody agreed to go. Thorne pushed his way back through the crowd and wearily mounted his played-out horse. There'd be no sleep for him for a while. Irritably he rode back toward the jail.

Part of the crowd followed him. One man said, "There's a U.S. marshal in town, sheriff, and a reporter from the *Rocky Mountain News.*"

"What the hell are they doing here?"

"Came to investigate that business down at the Indian camp."

Thorne cursed savagely, aloud this time. He knew that mess should have been cleaned up a long time ago. He'd intended to put pressure on those he knew had been involved to clean it up as soon as he got back. It hadn't occurred to him that the U.S. marshal's office in Denver would become involved so quickly. He'd thought there was plenty of time.

Apparently he had been wrong. Angrily he dismounted in front of the jail. To one of the men who had followed him he said, "Take my horse across to the stable, will you? Tell Donovan to give him a good rubdown, a little water and oats, and all the hay he can eat."

"Sure, Dave. You got any idea who might've killed Easterling?"

Dave Thorne didn't bother to answer that. He unlocked his office, went in, and slammed the door behind him. He supposed he'd have to see that goddamned U.S. marshal, but it would wait.

He opened the bottom drawer of his desk and took out a brown bottle of whiskey. There was a none-too-clean glass in the same drawer. He poured it half full and drank half of it at a gulp. It warmed him all the way down, so he drank the other half.

He fought down his irritation and bad temper, put his feet up on the desk, and contemplated the bottle and empty glass. Marcus Easterling had been well liked in Coyote Springs. As far as Dave knew, he hadn't had an enemy in town. There hadn't even been anyone who disliked him.

But he had been with the group that had attacked the Indian camp, and so his death had to, someway, be connected with that. The arrival of the U.S. marshal must have scared the hell out of everybody who had been part of it. Maybe Easterling had threatened to spill everything. Or maybe somebody had only thought he would.

He sat up and poured himself another drink, having discovered that the whiskey made him feel less tired. Gloomily he wondered how long it would be before he could go home and go to bed. He supposed he'd have to see the marshal first, and he ought to see Mrs. Easterling. He'd have to make some motions directed at finding out who had killed Marcus Easterling. Nobody would give a damn how tired he was.

The door opened as he downed his drink and Carl Brundage came in. "I heard that you were back."

Thorne scowled at him. "You know anything about Easterling?"

Brundage looked at him puzzledly. "Why should I?"

"He didn't have an enemy in the world. So it had to be connected with that stupid business down at the Indian camp."

"I wasn't in on that."

"I know you weren't." He stared at Brundage until Brundage lowered his glance. Then Thorne asked, "What do you want?"

"I want to talk to you about that business. And about that marshal and reporter who came in yesterday."

"What about them?"

"They got Orange and took him down there yesterday. They had him take pictures of everything."

Thorne said, "Oh, Christ!"

Brundage said, "I stuck my neck out and got into it. I took some of the men that did it out there last night and made them clean it up. We buried the bodies where they'll never be found, along with the shelters and lean-tos the Indians had. This morning I smashed Orange's photographic plates."

"But the marshal's got the prints?"

"Yes."

"Have you tried to get your hands on them?"

"You mean by going through his things?"

"What else?"

"No. I figured that was next."

"The marshal and the reporter saw the bodies and they can still testify, photographs or not."

Brundage said, "Not if they're dead."

Thorne stared at him disgustedly. "You've got a nerve coming down here and suggesting a double murder to me. I didn't arrest anybody for killing those Indians, but that don't mean I'll stand still for killing a U.S. marshal and a newspaperman."

"Have you got a better idea?"

"Sure. Let the ones who did the killing get arrested and go to trial."

"And let the whole damn thing get plastered over every front page in the country? You know what that will do to the town of Coyote Springs?"

"Maybe I don't give a damn. I can go someplace else."

"But I can't. I've got too much tied up here. Everything I own is invested here. Nobody knows this but me, and if you spill it, I'll have your hide, but the railroad has a line coming through here next year. It will mean that Coyote Springs will double or triple in size within a year."

"And you'll get rich."

"I'll make some money. Money I wouldn't mind sharing with whoever helps me keep the whole thing from blowing up."

Thorne stared at him. It was the first time in his life he had ever been offered a bribe. It took him by surprise, but he finally managed to ask, "You got an amount in mind?"

"No, but you think on it. I will too."

"If that marshal and reporter disappear, there will be half a dozen more marshals nosing around within two weeks."

Brundage said, "If I don't do the killing and you don't, they can't touch us. And the men who killed those Indians can't be any worse off than they already are."

Thorne said, "I'm so goddam tired I can't even think. Go up and see Mrs. Easterling for me. I've got to see that marshal, and then I'm going to bed. I haven't had any sleep for thirty-six hours."

Brundage nodded. He turned and went out, closing the door softly behind him. Thorne stared at it. Reluctantly he got to his feet, poured himself another drink, downed it, then went out the door, leaving it unlocked. There was only one place the U.S. marshal could be, and that was at the hotel. He walked up the street, climbed the steps to the veranda, crossed it, and went into the lobby. The clock over the clerk's desk said it was eleven o'clock.

Thorne asked, "Is he in his room?"

"Who?"

"That U.S. marshal," Thorne said irritably. "Who the hell did you think I was talking about?"

"Yeah. He's in his room. Number seven."

Thorne nodded shortly and headed for the stairs. He was a man of medium height, forty-seven years old, growing a little heavy now as he passed middle age. He had short-cut hair the color of straw and today a three-day growth of straw-colored whiskers on his sunburned face. His eyes were blue and hard. He was a humorless man, a widower, who would have courted Nora McKissick if he hadn't been so shy. So, instead of courting her, he took most of his meals at her restaurant and contented himself with watching her, something that made her nervous and made her dread his coming in.

He climbed the stairs heavily. He had been sheriff of Maxwell County for two terms and this fall would stand for re-election again, unopposed. He believed in the law, but he was also practical. He knew arresting seven men in a town this size and charging them with nine murders would cause headlines nationwide. The investigation and trial would turn into a three-ring circus because the victims had been Indians. So he'd tried to ignore what had happened. He'd tried to forget the bodies lying out there at the Indian camp, knowing that in time vultures and coyotes would pick them clean and scatter the bones. That, he knew now, had been the biggest mistake he'd ever made. If he'd had them buried and their lean-tos destroyed, he wouldn't be in this fix now.

He knocked on the door of Number 7, heard footsteps inside, and then the door was opened by a tall, lean man with a bony face, a wide mustache, and a gun in his hand. The man immediately put away the gun and said, "Come in. I've been wondering when you'd show up."

Thorne went in. He took off his hat and held it in both hands. This man was a United States marshal, and he was only sheriff of a small and remote county. He said, "I was up at the other end of the county serving eviction papers. I just got back."

"Do you know why I'm here?"

Thorne nodded. "To investigate the deaths of those Indians."

The marshal was looking at him with ill-concealed disapproval. He said, "My name's Cole. Frank Cole. I'm out of the Denver office."

"Dave Thorne." Thorne stuck out his hand and the marshal took it and then let it go. Cole didn't say anything, so Thorne said lamely, "Hell, man, they was only Indians. Can you imagine the stink there'd be if I arrested eight or ten men in a town this size and charged them with killin' that bunch of unarmed Indians?"

"That's your job, isn't it?"

"I work for the people of this county. The white people. They're the ones that elect me, and their taxes pay my salary. What the hell do them Indians pay? Nothing. That's what they pay. Besides, after what they done to General Custer and his boys at the Little Big Horn—well, maybe they got just what was coming to them."

"They weren't even from the same tribe. And they weren't at the Little Big Horn."

"Hell, Injuns are all alike." Thorne was losing his temper under Cole's unconcealed disapproval.

Cole shrugged, seeing plainly that he was getting no place with this man. He asked, "You're going to investigate Mr. Easterling's murder, aren't you?"

"Of course I am! But, mister, I been in the saddle the whole damn night. I haven't slept since night before last. I'm going home now and I'm going to bed. I'll probably see you tomorrow."

Cole said, "Then I take it I can expect no help from you in this Indian thing."

"No sir, you can't. In fact, I'd like to give you a little advice. You go on back to Denver and forget about them Indians. Otherwise, you're likely to join 'em, wherever they are."

He backed to the door, putting on his hat. He opened it, but, before he stepped out into the hall, he said, "Whoever it was in this town that killed them Injuns—well, they ain't going to prison for a thing like that."

"Then, you know who they are?"

"No, I don't know who they are. But I do know this. If they can kill Injuns, they can kill a U.S. marshal. And a reporter too." He stepped into the hall, slamming the door angrily.

Cole stared at the door. He had hoped for some cooperation from the local sheriff. It appeared he would get none. He shrugged faintly. He'd just have to do it all by himself. The sheriff could not, at least, refuse him the use of the county jail.

CHAPTER 11

Reed Sheridan was a tall, morose-looking man with straight yellowish hair that was usually too long, and a sparse mustache, the hairs of which always seemed to be going in different directions. He was the town lawyer, but because neither the town nor the county had enough legal business to support a lawyer, he also owned and operated the abstract company, called the Maxwell County Abstract Company. He had a two-story brown frame house half a block from the creek, a plump wife, and two grade-school boys.

He had something else, a memory that even now, eleven years after the end of the war, still tormented him. He sat in his office, looking down out the window into the street, and thought about Marcus Easterling with a smashed skull lying in the widow Wallace's stable. And he was scared, scared the way he had been that day at Gettysburg, wanting to run again but now not knowing where to run and unable to anyway because of his wife and kids and his place in this community.

But the panic was the same. The raw, cold fear of death that came over you like a chill and set you to trembling and changed your will from that of a man into something craven that could do nothing but surrender to an irresistible urge to survive.

That was the kind of panic that had taken control of him at Gettysburg. He could still see it as plainly as if it had been yesterday, the rain misting down and the powder-smoke haze drifting through the woods and the gray men coming out of that smoke with their muskets held at the ready.

His regiment's orders had been to hold, and maybe they would have held, except that suddenly there was an awful, unearthly sound, a screech, a rebel yell, as the gray-clad men came rolling forward, double-timing now, screaming like demons out of hell.

They were well dug in, and well armed, and there were enough of them to have stopped the charge and rolled it back. But suddenly Reed Sheridan felt panic seize him and lost control of himself and his actions. Then he was up from behind the breastworks, running, running. . . .

Running away from that line of gray-clad men. When he jumped up and ran, the same panic seized others close to him, and they jumped up and also ran. In only a few short minutes the whole dug-in line was running, and men were falling as the rebels stopped, and knelt, and laid a deadly fire into the ranks of the fleeing Union troops.

Reed Sheridan was never brought to trial for cowardice. Everyone had fled, and no one had said that Reed Sheridan was the first, without whom it might not have happened at all.

But Reed Sheridan knew. And he wondered how many men lay dead or were permanently crippled because of him. Fifty? A hundred? A thousand? Men who, had they stayed behind their breastworks and fought, might have rolled back the long gray line.

There were no battles after that. Not for Reed Sheridan. Not for his regiment. Half of them came down with the dysentery and the whole regiment was sent to the rear, and while they'd later gotten near enough to hear the guns, they had never again been called upon to fight.

So there had been no opportunity for Reed Sheridan to redeem himself. His own conception of himself at the war's end was that he was a coward, who ran when he should have stood fast and whose running had started the panic that led to a general rout of the whole regiment.

His wife didn't know. Nor did his sons. Nor did anybody else. But Reed Sheridan knew. And he let the knowing go on tormenting him.

At least he had until the day Pat Mosely rode into town yelling that there was a camp of dirty, murdering Indians out along the creek. Suddenly that became an opportunity for Sheridan to go into battle and to finally redeem himself. At the same time, he could strike a blow for Colonel Custer and his gallant men, dead on a remote battlefield.

Eagerly he had gone home for his horse. Eagerly he had gotten out his hunting rifle. He had hesitated about the saber, but finally had strapped that on too. And he'd ridden down to the Drovers Saloon and joined the other men and ridden out of town and along the two-track wagon road to the Indian camp.

Once, during that five- or six-mile ride, he had felt the

cold fist of fear in his gut, because he knew neither how many Indians there were nor how well armed, but this time he was able to control the fear and make it go away, and it was a Reed Sheridan who had finally triumphed over his own fear that finally rode into the pitiful Indian camp.

Reed Sheridan had, that day, proved to himself that a single act of cowardice does not a coward make. But the price had been too high. He had made a killer of himself. And now he was faced either with going to trial for murder or joining the others in doing whatever was needed to make sure the law couldn't send them all off to prison for the crimes. But the thought of Easterling's death threw him into panic.

Suddenly he got up out of his chair. He was a close friend of Art Ohlman, and because he needed someone to talk to who had the same problem he did, he thought of Art Ohlman first.

He closed and locked his door and went down the outside stairway, putting on his hat. Most of the people who normally would have been on the street were crowded up at the widow Wallace's stable, or helping take Marcus Easterling's body to the undertaker's, or at Easterling's house trying to convey their sympathy to a confused and hysterical Mrs. Easterling.

He noticed, as he headed for Art Ohlman's barbershop, that the Drovers Saloon was still open. The meeting behind Brundage's store had been adjourned as soon as the yelling in the street had told them of the murder of Marcus Easterling.

Walking, Sheridan remembered that Welch had been the last one to arrive. He had been sent after Tolliver, Easterling, and Olivera. Shortly thereafter, Tolliver and Olivera had arrived, followed somewhat later by Welch. Easterling never had showed up.

He arrived at Ohlman's barbershop and went inside. Ohlman had no customers, either in front, where he shaved and cut hair, or in back, where there were tubs for baths. Ohlman was sitting in the barber chair holding a newspaper, but he wasn't reading it. Sheridan closed the door.

Ohlman nodded at him. "Awful about Marcus Easterling, wasn't it?"

Sheridan nodded.

"Who do you think killed him, anyway?"

Sheridan said, "Art, both you and me *know* who killed him. Marcus must have balked at going any farther trying to hide what happened out at the Indian camp. Tod Welch smashed his head in when he refused to come to the meeting in the back room of Brundage's store."

There was a worried frown on Art Ohlman's face. He nodded. "Nobody else *could* have done it, could they? All of us were there in Brundage's store. Except for Tolliver, Olivera, and Juan Salgado."

"Neither Tolliver nor Salgado was even in on the trouble at the Indian camp. Salgado claimed his horse was lame and never even left town. Tolliver stopped before we got there. So neither of them would have any reason to kill Easterling, and I can't see Olivera doing it."

"So suppose it was Welch? The sheriff will find out."

"How? Welch will expect every one of us to swear he was there in Brundage's store."

"How can he do that? Without letting the U.S. marshal know we were having a meeting? And if the marshal knows we were meeting and knows everyone that was there, then he'll have a list of all those who were at the Indian camp."

Sheridan sat down in one of the straight-backed chairs placed with their backs to the window for waiting customers. "What in the hell got into us that day?" he asked despairingly. "I shot helpless people that didn't even have any guns. I saw you empty your gun into that woman in the canvas lean-to. What made us do something as awful as that?"

Ohlman's face lost color at Sheridan's mention of the woman. There was no friendship in his voice as he replied, "You were seeing things if you think you saw me do that! What the hell kind of a thing is that to say, anyhow? I thought you were my friend!"

Sheridan stared with amazement at Ohlman's face. Sheridan immediately understood that he would be extremely unwise to pursue it further. He looked at Ohlman helplessly and asked, "What are we going to do?"

"Leave it to Brundage and Welch, I guess. And keep our damn mouths shut about it unless we want to end up like Marcus Easterling."

Sheridan nodded. He got up, opened the door, and stood in it a moment, wondering what else there was to say. There wasn't anything. He nodded at Ohlman, turned, and headed for his office again.

He had won a victory over himself out at the Indian camp, a victory long overdue, but the cost was exorbitant.

Ohlman stared at the door after Sheridan had closed it. He had been friends with Sheridan for years, but suddenly he felt a violent dislike for him.

His face contorted and he lowered it into his hands. He sat like that for a long time. Then, abruptly, he got up, pulled the shades in front of the windows, locked the door, and placed the CLOSED sign on the window sill. The way he felt today he didn't want to talk to anybody. Besides, his hands were shaking so badly he'd probably cut somebody's throat if he tried to give him a shave.

He went back and got up into the barber chair again. The sun shone against the shades, giving the room a warm and pleasant glow. But all Ohlman was seeing was that woman, sitting in her lean-to, screaming, screaming. . . .

The shrillness of the screams had triggered something inside of him, something over which he'd had absolutely no control. Suddenly, instead of an Indian woman, it had been Marian there in front of him, and he had a gun, and it was his chance to silence her shrill, screaming, harridan's voice once and for all.

He had no memory of the individual shots. He had just fired, and worked the action, and fired again, and worked the action, and fired again . . . until the gun was empty. The baby had been squalling, and Tod Welch had silenced it with a single bullet. By then the rest of it was over. Something over and done that can never be reversed.

Maybe they were all going to have to pay the price for what they'd done. Marcus Easterling had already paid.

Ohlman realized, without quite understanding it, that he had been killing his wife out at that Indian camp. He'd had no reason to empty his gun into an unarmed Indian woman even if she had been screaming with fear. He thought about that for a while. He should have walked out on Marian years ago. He should have taken a horse some night and ridden away and kept going until a thousand miles and a brand new identity separated them forever.

But he hadn't, and now it was too late. If he tried to run now, the law would come after him.

He thought about how much he hated her. Then, surprisingly, he thought about how much he'd loved her when they first were married. And he wondered how, in the space of hardly more than seven years, love turns to hate.

She had been to blame. By belittling. By sneering at his being a barber instead of something else. By complaining constantly that he didn't bring enough money home. Even by sneering at the way he performed with her in bed, until it got so he couldn't perform at all.

God damn her, he thought. And damn me for a fool because I shot a helpless Indian woman instead of shooting Marian. The price for shooting either would probably have been the same. And how much satisfaction it would have given him to shoot Marian instead of shooting that Indian.

He began to think about that, about actually shooting Marian. They couldn't hang a man but once. They didn't send you to prison any longer for two killings than for one. And even if they did . . . what kind of life did he have now? What kind of life would he have in the future?

He got up and began pacing nervously back and forth, like a cat in a cage. A couple of times, he stopped and held his hands up before his face. The first time, they were still trembling violently. The second, they were steady as a rock.

Tonight, he thought, he wasn't going home. He was

going to the saloon and he was going to get drunk. That was the first decision, a minor one.

The second was more serious. If it appeared that he was going to be arrested for participating in that business out at the Indian camp . . . well, he was going to kill Marian. And after that they could do to him whatever they damned pleased.

CHAPTER 12

As soon as everyone had left, Brundage opened the door between the back room and the front part of his store. Ina Blair was standing in the front doorway looking into the street. There were no customers in the store. Ina turned. "Did you hear what happened to Mr. Easterling?"

Brundage nodded. "A terrible thing. Terrible!"

"Who could have done it? Do you know of any strangers in town?"

"Only that U.S. marshal and the reporter from the *News.*"

"They wouldn't kill someone."

"If they're really who they say they are." Brundage didn't elaborate, but stepped past Ina into the street. He knew Ina to be one of the worst gossips in town. His casual remark would have been spread all over town by noon.

He crossed the street to the Drovers Saloon. Welch would be there, and Brundage wanted to talk with him.

Welch was tending bar. Howie was finishing up the cleaning chores that Brundage had interrupted earlier.

There was a crowd in the saloon, a big crowd for this time of day, all talking about the murder of Marcus Easterling. As Brundage pushed through the crowd, someone asked, "Did you hear about Mr. Easterling, Mr. Brundage?"

He nodded. "An awful thing. I hope the sheriff catches whoever did it right away."

"Who you think it might have been?"

Brundage shrugged. "There aren't any strangers in town, except for that marshal and the newspaper reporter."

"You don't think it was them?"

"Not if they're who they say they are." He pushed on to the bar. Welch brought out his private bottle and a glass. Brundage poured himself a drink. "I want to talk to you. But not right here. After a bit I'll go out back like I was going to the outhouse. We can talk in the back room."

Welch nodded. Brundage sipped his whiskey. He finished the first drink and poured himself another, listening to the talk. He heard one man say that he'd bet Easterling had threatened to go to the U.S. marshal with the truth about what had happened at the Indian camp, but nobody seemed to agree with him. Brundage felt himself relax.

He shoved the bottle toward Welch, got up, and went through the door leading to the back room. The outhouse was in the yard beyond, but he did not go through the outside door.

After several minutes, Welch came from the saloon, closed the door behind him, and dropped the bar into place. He wouldn't quite meet Brundage's angry eyes. Brundage said, "You did it, didn't you?"

Welch scowled straight at him now, and once more Brundage felt a twinge of fear. Welch was dangerous. But Brundage didn't look away. He persisted, "You did, didn't you?"

"The son of a bitch was getting ready to blab."

"How do you know that? He was in it right along with the rest of you. Why should he blab?"

"He wouldn't come to that meeting in the back room of your store. And you said it yourself: if we don't hang together, we'll hang separately."

"Thorne can't overlook Easterling's death. He'll have to investigate it."

Welch shrugged. "Nobody saw me."

"You just think nobody saw you. What if somebody did?"

Welch's eyes were growing ever angrier. "What the hell do you want me to do about it now? It's done."

Brundage realized he had been taking his own fear out on Welch. Besides, the man was right. It was done. It could not be changed. Anyway, maybe there was something to be gained by it. Maybe others, such as Howie Bracken, Cliff Tolliver, and Juan Salgado, would take a lesson from Easterling's death. Maybe they'd be just scared enough to keep their mouths shut as long as the marshal was in town.

Brundage said, "All right. It's done. Let's just go on from here."

"And do what?"

"First, we've got to get those photographs."

"You want me to take care of that?"

Brundage shook his head. "No. But I'll need you for a

lookout. This noon, when Cole goes to dinner, I'll go through his room. I want you to be standing in front of the saloon. If he starts coming back, just go into the saloon and I'll get the hell out of his room."

"What if he eats in the hotel?"

"I don't think he will. Jackson gave him a hard time last night. And besides, I think he's got his eye on Nora McKissick. He had breakfast there, and he was there a damn long time."

Welch nodded. "All right."

Brundage went out the back door, circled around the side of the saloon, and crossed the street to his store. Welch unbarred the door and re-entered the saloon. He hadn't been behind the bar very long before Art Ohlman came in. He came to the end of the bar and Welch moved down there to wait on him. Ohlman said, "Juan Salgado's getting ready to leave town."

"How do you know that?"

"He's carrying stuff from the house to the stable. I figure he's loading his wagon in the stable, and as soon as it's dark, he'll hitch up and drive out of town."

Welch nodded. "All right."

"What are we going to do?"

"Do? Nothing. Why should we do anything?"

Ohlman looked disappointed. He finished his drink and left hastily.

Welch watched him leave, automatically going about the business of tending bar. He heard the talk, and sometimes spoke to someone, but his mind wasn't really on it. He was thinking about Salgado, who had agreed to go on the Indian raid but who hadn't shown up and had later claimed his horse was lame.

Easterling's death must have frightened the man. Scared him bad enough to make him give up everything and leave.

He forced his thoughts back to the U.S. marshal that was in town. Brundage's plan for getting the photographs out of Cole's room at the hotel was good. Welch didn't see how the marshal could make a case if he didn't have the photographs. The Indians' bodies had been buried and the Indian campsite had been cleaned up.

But if just one person lost his nerve . . . as Easterling had been about to do . . . as Salgado was apparently doing now, then the marshal would have a witness, someone who could name names and affirm that a massacre had taken place.

Well, he thought, Salgado was only loading his wagon now. He wouldn't dare leave town until it got dark. There was plenty of time to do what must be done.

Frank Cole sat at the window of his hotel room, hidden by the curtains, staring down into the street. He was a little uncertain as to how he should now proceed. The safest way, of course, would be to get off a telegram to Denver and ask for help. But he hesitated about doing that, mostly because of pride. He hated to admit that he couldn't handle a job he had been sent to do.

There was a knock on the door. He crossed the room and unlocked it, and Flagg stepped into the room. "Did you hear about that murder?"

Cole nodded.

Flagg said, "I was over at the undertaker's and saw the body. The killer damn near knocked the poor man's head off."

Cole shrugged.

"Do you think the dead man was one of those who killed all of those Indians?"

"I know he was."

"Then, his murder was probably connected with that."

"Likely was."

"Then, you think he was getting ready to talk?"

"Why else would they kill him?"

Flagg said, "I've been writing my story. Describing what we saw down at that Indian camp."

Cole saw Nora McKissick come around the corner half a block up the street. She stayed on the far side of the street, but when she came abreast of the hotel, she turned her head and glanced up at the window of his room. He started to push the curtains aside, then changed his mind. Nora kept looking at his window long enough so that he knew her glance was more than casual.

Brief excitement touched him and then quickly went away. Nora McKissick wasn't the kind of woman to give him that kind of encouragement. Certainly not this soon. No, it was something else. For some reason, Nora McKissick wanted to talk to him.

He pulled his hunting-case watch from his pocket. It was a little after eleven, too early to go to the restaurant for dinner. He would have to wait. He watched her go on down the street and enter her tiny restaurant, thinking, "That's a damn fine woman, and a handsome one, and you'd better stay around here long enough so that when you go you can take her along with you."

Putting it so definitely, even in his thoughts, surprised him, but, then, he'd never met a woman like Nora McKissick before.

Flagg had followed the direction of his glance and had seen Nora look up at his room. He said, "Beautiful woman, isn't she?"

Cole nodded absently.

Flagg seemed to forget Nora. He was now looking curiously around Cole's room. I can't figure out where you hid those photographs. At least, not any place where they wouldn't be found."

Cole said, "Anything that can be hidden can be found."

"I'll bet you didn't hide them in this room at all."

Cole grinned at him. "Go back to your story. Are you going to interview Mrs. Easterling?"

Flagg nodded. "This afternoon."

"Let me know what she says, if you think it's anything that might help point to her husband's killer."

Flagg said, "All right," and stepped out of the room. Cole closed and locked the door. He wanted to be able to watch the street without having to worry about somebody busting in unexpectedly and maybe taking a shot at him.

He made himself comfortable, waiting, but he glanced at his watch every five minutes or so. Once, he put it to his ear to make sure it hadn't stopped. At last, at a quarter of twelve, he got up, put on his hat, and left the room. He walked slowly, as if in no hurry. He crossed the lobby, went out onto the veranda, then headed down the street.

By now most of the crowds had disappeared. Many had gone home for dinner, he supposed. Or back to their jobs, whatever they might happen to be. Easterling's body was at the undertaker's. Someone, he thought, should have seen the killer, since it apparently had happened that morning in broad daylight.

He reached the restaurant and went inside. That early, there were no other customers, but he doubted if the place would be empty long. Nora McKissick came from the kitchen, unsmiling, scared. She said, "I wanted to talk to you, and I hoped you'd understand when I looked up at your room."

Cole said, "Go ahead."

"It's about the Salgado family. They're packing all their things into a wagon they have hidden in the stable, and I think they're planning to leave town tonight."

"Why? Was Salgado in on that business at the Indian camp?"

"No. He changed his mind, his wife said, at the last minute, and he later told the others that his horse was lame." By way of explanation she added, "I live right next door to them."

"Then, he probably knows who the others were. And Easterling's murder scared him."

"I think that's it. I tried to speak to Mrs. Salgado this morning but she avoided me."

Cole said, "The most dangerous thing he could do right now is try leaving town."

"That's what I thought. That's why—" She stopped as the door opened. She said, "There is beef stew and chicken with dumplings."

Cole said, "Chicken with dumplings."

Nora McKissick glanced at the man who had come in the door and smiled. Then she disappeared into the kitchen, to return a moment later with two cups of coffee, one for Cole and one for the newcomer, whom Cole had never seen before.

He waited for his meal, and watched her appreciatively whenever she appeared. Once, she caught him doing it and flushed, but he could tell that she was not displeased.

He wished he knew what he was going to do. He wished he had the willing co-operation of the sheriff. His coming seemed to have precipitated all kinds of things. And he had the uneasy feeling that the trouble had just begun.

CHAPTER 13

Frank Cole sat at the counter long after he had finished his meal. Nora McKissick kept refilling his coffee cup until the routine became ridiculous and they both began having trouble keeping their faces straight each time she did. At last it became apparent that the place was not going to empty out and give him a chance to be alone with her. He paid the bill, and as she took the money he said, "I'm going to be up around Salgado's house this evening when he leaves. Will it be all right if I stop and talk to you?"

"I won't be through here until nearly eight."

"Then, I'll meet you here and walk you home."

She nodded, her expression reflecting a fleeting concern as to the speed with which he was pressing her. But her smile, though faint, was genuine, and he knew she liked him and wanted to see him again.

Going out the door, he reflected upon her still being single. Certainly she had not remained so for lack of opportunities to remarry. She must simply not have found anyone with whom she wanted to spend the rest of her life. He wondered how she would feel about him when she got to know him. Would she turn away from him, or would she come away with him? The answer to that question, he realized suddenly, was very important to him in spite of the fact that he had seen her only twice.

Glancing across the street, he saw Tod Welch disappearing into the swinging doors of his saloon. He went on to the hotel and climbed the stairs to his room.

Flagg was just coming out of his room down the hall. He asked, "Forget something?"

Cole looked at him with puzzlement. "What makes you ask that?"

"I thought I just heard your door close." Flagg shrugged. "I think I'll get something to eat."

Cole unlocked the door and went into his room. He stopped just inside and stared. The mattress lay on the floor on top of a pile of bedclothes. The drawers of the dresser had been emptied out, as had Cole's carpetbag. The carpet had been thrown back, revealing a liberal layer of dust that had been beneath it, and the room was generally a mess.

He glanced instantly at the window shade. It was still in place, apparently undisturbed. He did not cross the room to it, knowing that his window was probably being watched and doing so would only give away his hiding place.

The ransacking of his room came as no surprise. He had expected it. He turned, went back down into the lobby, and crossed to the desk. Today, the same man who had tried to refuse him service in the dining room was behind the desk. Cole said, "My room has been ransacked. It was locked. How do you suppose whoever did it got in?"

The man behind the desk couldn't meet his glance. "You must have forgotten to lock it, Mr. Cole."

Cole knew there was no use pursuing it further. The hotel manager had given a key to someone, but he'd never get him to admit it. He said, "Get a maid up there to clean things up."

"Yes sir. Right away." The man called to someone at the rear of the lobby, beckoning. A Mexican woman came shuffling to the desk, and the hotel manager said, "Mr. Cole's room had been broken into. Please go up immediately and clean and straighten it."

The woman nodded. She disappeared momentarily, returning with broom, bucket, mop, and dustpan. She crossed the lobby and climbed the stairs.

So far, Cole had faces but few names. Tod Welch was one he knew had participated in the killings at the Indian camp. Easterling had been another one, but Easterling was dead. The helper at the saloon had, that first day, looked at him as though he wanted to talk to him but Cole knew instinctively that Easterling's death would have scared any such notions out of him.

But there was Salgado, who was leaving town because he was scared. There might be something there. . . .

He looked at the man behind the desk. If he asked directions to Salgado's house he would put the man in further danger. But Nora McKissick lived next door. He asked, "Where does Mrs. McKissick live?"

The hotel manager had a half smirk on his face as he glanced up. "A block up, two blocks to the right. Small yellow frame house that faces east."

Cole nodded. "Thanks."

"Mighty handsome woman, Mrs. McKissick. Lost her brother with Custer at the Little Big Horn."

"Yes. Thank you." Cole went out and stood for a moment on the hotel veranda. There were a couple of old men sunning themselves in creaking wicker rockers. They stared at him with open curiosity. Finally, just as Cole was about to step off the veranda, one of them asked in a cracked voice, "What you goin' to do if you find them fellers, mister? You're a federal marshal, ain't ye?"

Cole nodded, not committing himself, wondering as he crossed the dusty street about Nora's first husband and what had happened to him. And how long ago. He thought about her face and those lovely gray eyes and her mouth, and then he saw in his mind the way she walked, her fine shoulders and straight back and her rounded and provocative hips.

He walked up the street to the first intersection, turned right, and walked another block and a half until he spotted a single-story yellow house facing east.

He stopped in the shade of a huge cottonwood, fairly sure he was being observed, yet, as he turned and searched the street behind him, seeing no one.

Half a dozen quick steps put him into the alley and out of sight of whoever might have been watching him. There was a house on either side of Nora McKissick's, but only one had a stable behind it. At a fast walk, almost a run, he reached the stable, opened one of the big rear doors slightly, and squeezed inside.

A wagon took up half the stable. In the other half there were three saddle horses. At the moment, no one was in the stable, but the wagon was already piled high with household goods.

Cole edged around the wagon and peered out the open door leading to the yard and the house beyond. He saw a middle-aged, dark-skinned man come from the back porch of the house. The man stepped into the stable before he saw Cole. When he did, he started violently.

Cole nodded. "Good afternoon, Mr. Salgado."

"You're that marshal, ain't you?"

"Yes sir, I am. I'd like to ask you a question or two."

"No time to talk to you."

"Are you leaving town? Mr. Easterling's death scare you away?"

Salgado put the box he was carrying into the wagon. When he turned, his eyes were scared. He said, "You're damned right it did. I'm getting the hell out of here before the same thing happens to me."

"Leaving might bring it on. You know too much. You know the names of every man who went down to that Indian camp."

"I wasn't in on it. Anybody will tell you. My horse was lame."

"But you know the names. And they'll kill you for that."

"Not if I don't tell, they won't." Salgado's face, normally dark, was sallow and pale, as though he was sick at his stomach.

"Whether you tell or not. Easterling didn't tell anything. But he got killed."

"How'd you know I was getting ready to leave?"

"Mrs. McKissick told me. She said she thought you were in danger because of it."

Sweating, Salgado removed his hat and ran his fingers through his hair. He leaned against the doorjamb. There was a kind of fatalism in his face suddenly, as if he had accepted the fact that he was probably going to be killed no matter what he did.

Cole said, "I know the faces. I followed them out there last night when they hauled the bodies away and buried them. All I need is the names." He felt no guilt over asking for the names. Telling them would put Salgado in no worse danger than he was already in. Leaving had been his mistake. Even with the wagon hidden in the stable, there was no concealing the movements back and forth between the stable and the house.

Salgado shrugged. "All right. Pat Mosely brought the news. Reed Sheridan went along, and Art Ohlman and Tod Welch. There was Cliff Tolliver and Pete Olivera and Marcus Easterling. Oh, and Howie Bracken. Tod Welch closed the saloon."

Cole said, "Eight men, then. I only saw seven out there cleaning up last night, and Brundage was one of them. Wasn't he in on it?"

Salgado shook his head. "He's probably just interested in keeping it from getting out. Keeping it out of the newspapers. Maybe he figures that with no bodies how are you going to prove anything."

"Two men didn't go out and help clean up the Indian camp. Have any idea who they might have been?"

"Howie Bracken was probably one of them. He'd have stayed behind to look after the saloon. The other was likely Tolliver. I heard that he balked before they ever got to the Indian camp. Welch had a run-in with him and knocked him down. That Welch is a mean one."

"Do you think that he was the one who killed Easterling?"

"Who else could have done such a thing?"

Cole nodded. "All right. I think I've got everything I need. Will you drop me a line when you get where you're going? I'll need you to testify. Just send it to me, Frank Cole, at the U.S. marshal's office in Denver."

"I don't know. . . ."

Cole asked, "Was your horse really lame?"

Salgado shook his head. "My wife talked me out of going. Not that it was hard. I didn't really want to go anyway. I didn't have anything against those Indians. They had nothing to do with what happened in June at the Little Big Horn."

Cole heard a scuffing step behind Salgado and raised his glance. He saw a plump, dark-skinned woman coming down the path carrying an armload of pots and pans. When she saw him, her eyes turned scared.

Cole said, "I'll be leaving. I'll try to find Welch and put him in jail. I don't think anybody else will bother you, but be careful until you are well out of town."

He edged past the wagon and went out into the alley the same way he had come in. He had the names. If he found Welch and lodged him in the county jail, then Salgado would probably be safe. The others might have participated in the killings at the Indian camp, but he doubted if any but Welch was capable of cold-blooded murder. At least not yet.

He hurried down the alley and back toward the main street of the town. He headed straight for the Drovers Saloon.

Welch wasn't there, and a scared Howie Bracken said he didn't know where he was. Cole crossed the street to Brundage's Mercantile, where the story was the same. From Brundage he got directions to Tod Welch's house and headed for it, hurrying.

Halfway there, he heard the boom of a shotgun, dull with distance, almost a thump.

He whirled and ran toward the sound. He didn't even have to guess what had happened.

He should have stayed with Salgado instead of going to look for Welch. Whatever had happened was his fault.

No. It was not his fault. He couldn't have guarded Salgado forever. His best chance of saving the man's life had been in finding and jailing Welch.

But Welch had acted first. And, because there had been only one shot, he knew that Juan Salgado was dead, even before he heard the widow's screams of grief.

CHAPTER 14

Several townspeople had reached the Salgado house before Cole could. He ran in the back gate and pushed on through. Mrs. Salgado was on the ground beside her husband, whose chest was a welter of clotting blood. She was hysterical. The kids stood twenty or thirty feet away, close together, white-faced and scared, not yet crying.

Cole knelt beside Mrs. Salgado. "Who did it? Did you see?"

She stared blankly at him. He repeated the question firmly. She dumbly shook her head.

She recognized him then, and for an instant she seemed to forget her dead husband on the ground. With bitterness, she cried, "It is your fault! If you had stayed away . . . if you had let him alone. . . ."

Cole said, "He was leaving town. That's why he was killed. He was leaving town."

He knew she did not believe that. Nor did any of the others at whom he looked as he got to his feet. In the eyes of these townspeople, he had brought the trouble simply by coming here. They did not blame the ones who had gone out to the Indian camp and slaughtered the Indians. They did not even blame whichever of them had killed both Easterling and Salgado. They blamed Frank Cole, and Flagg, both of whom had stirred all this trouble up by coming here.

He saw Nora McKissick running along the alley, holding up her skirts. She went past him, and immediately to Mrs. Salgado. She raised her gently to her feet and led her to the house. She spoke to the children and they followed her.

Someone in the crowd, a woman, followed them in and came out a few moments later with a blanket, which she laid over the corpse. Someone else went after the sheriff and Norman Reeves and his hearse.

There was nothing more Cole could do, but he waited, hoping Nora McKissick would come out. The crowd kept growing, and everyone who came looked at him with open hostility, as if he were the killer himself.

He knew it was impossible that everyone in town approved of the killing at the Indian camp. But everyone in town resented him and blamed him for the two killings that had happened since he arrived.

A couple of other women, friends of the Salgados, went in the back door, and a few minutes later, Nora McKissick came out. She walked past the blanket-covered body without looking at it and joined Frank Cole at the back gate. He said, "They blame me."

"They need someone to blame. You're a stranger, so you're the logical choice." Her face was very pale. He wanted to touch her, to put his arm around her, but he did not, fearing that she might misunderstand.

"I've got to get him and put him in jail."

"Who?"

"Welch. He's got to be the one."

"Do you know all of them?"

He nodded. "Mr. Salgado gave me the names and the corroboration I needed. I saw the faces last night at the Indian camp when they all went out to bury the bodies and clean up the place. I still need an eyewitness or someone who will testify against them. Failing that, I'll have to piece together all the evidence I have to build a strong case."

"What are you going to do now?"

"Well, the sheriff won't help me, so I suppose I'd better send a telegram to Denver and get some deputies."

"How long will that take?"

"Three days, at least."

"A lot can happen in three days." She turned her head, looked up, and met his glance head on. "Be careful. He has killed twice. He will try killing you."

"I have been in bad places before."

They walked in silence several minutes, reached the main street, and turned into it. Cole said, "You're seeing me will not help your business."

She did not reply.

Cole looked down at her, keeping his glance steadily on her face until the force of it made her raise her own. She flushed faintly, but her eyes did not waver. Cole said, "You know how I feel toward you. It is too soon to be saying it, but I have a feeling there is not going to be much time. Give a thought to leaving here with me."

She made no protest, because there was no coquettishness in her. She only nodded, and when they reached the door of her small restaurant, went inside, faintly frowning, without looking at him again.

He pulled his watch from his pocket and glanced at it. It was nearly two o'clock. Plenty of time to get a telegram to Denver, to the United States marshal's office before it closed.

The telegraph office was not next to the hotel, the way he might have expected. It was down the street, next to the livery barn, in a small frame building over which hung a weathered sign that said WELLS FARGO and beneath that a smaller, newer sign that said WESTERN UNION. He walked that way, noting the poles that led the wires to the telegraph office and then went on, up through town and toward Denver, more than two hundred miles away.

When he reached the place, he discovered that, in addition to being the telegraph office, the building also housed the U. S. Post Office. The man inside was the same one who had appeared when the coach came in yesterday and who had exchanged mailbags with the driver. He still wore the same green eyeshade, and he still seemed just as nervous as he had the first time Cole saw him.

Across the room there was a desk, with wires, batteries, and telegraph paraphernalia. Over there also, the telegraph instrument clicked monotonously. Traffic not concerned with Coyote Springs, Cole supposed, because the operator paid no attention to it.

Cole said, "I want to send a telegram."

"Yes sir." The man was as nervous as if Cole were serving a warrant on him. With shaking hands, he shoved a yellow pad and pencil at Cole. Cole quickly wrote out his message. "Request two deputies immediately. Urgent." He signed his name.

The man read the message, becoming even more agitated. Cole would have suspected him of being guilty of something if he hadn't known otherwise. The telegrapher crossed to the instrument and sat down at it. He waited several moments, until it was still, then began tapping on the key.

Suddenly he stopped and turned his head to look at Cole with puzzlement. "It's dead."

No longer was there any chattering from the instrument. Cole asked, "How much of it did you get sent?"

"Just the heading, I'm afraid."

"By heading you mean the address?"

"Yes sir."

"And none of the message itself?"

"Just the first word, 'Request.'"

"Why, do you think, it went dead? Does it do that often?"

"No sir. It never has before. Except once, during a bad storm, when the lines were down."

"All right. If it comes to life again, get my message off."

"Yes sir."

"What time does the mail leave for Denver?"

"Twice a week, sir. When the stage comes through."

"And that won't be for two more days?"

"That's right, sir."

"All right." Cole went out. On the walk in front of the telegraph office he stared at the lines leading away from it both north and south. He could see no cut line.

Someone must have seen him go into the telegraph office. That someone must have hastily cut the line. So it couldn't be too far from here. He could ride north, find the break, and splice it together again. If he could find some wire and if he could climb the poles.

Except that he knew it would be no use. He couldn't watch every mile of line. The instant he headed out to find the break, whoever had cut it in the first place would cut it someplace else.

He headed for the hotel. His room had been cleaned up, the bed put back together. The contents of his carpetbag lay spread out on the bed, along with the bag itself.

Howie Bracken was in the room, looking like a cornered rabbit, trembling the same way. Cole looked at the scared little man, thinking that there were all kinds of courage in the world and that Howie had more than his share of it, coming here when he knew two men had already died because of the danger they were to Welch and the others.

Cole said, "Mr. Bracken, isn't it?"

"Yes sir." Howie's voice was weak. He sounded as scared as he looked.

"I hope you came up the back way and that nobody saw you."

"I did. And I don't think I was seen."

"You want to see me about the killings, don't you? I saw the way you looked at me yesterday in the saloon."

"Yes sir. I rode out there with them but I quit before the killing started."

"All right." Cole got paper and a pencil out of the things lying on the bed. "You don't mind giving me a written statement?"

Howie looked as if he was going to run.

"It won't be used, it won't even be known about, until every one of them is safely in jail."

Howie nodded. Cole sat down and swiftly wrote out a brief statement. He put down the names Salgado had given him and handed the paper to Howie. The man looked embarrassed. "I can't read, sir."

"I'll read it to you, then." Cole did. He asked, when he had finished, "Is that right? Is everything correct?"

"Yes sir. Those are the ones."

"Will you sign it, then?"

Again Howie looked embarrassed. "I can't write, sir."

"Then, make a mark and I'll witness it."

Howie made a laborious X at the bottom of the page. Cole dated and signed as a witness to the "signature."

Cole said, "One more thing," as Howie headed for the door. "Who started it? After you all got out there, I mean? Who changed it from just 'chasing the Indians off' to killing them?"

"Mr. Welch, sir. He fired the first shot. Then everyone was shooting. One of the Indians had an old gun, but he never fired it."

"All right. Let me look out into the hall and be sure it's clear before you leave." He opened the door and stepped out into the hall. There was no one in sight. He beckoned Howie and preceded him down the hall to the back stairs. There still was no one in sight.

He knew that going farther with Howie would only expose him to greater risk. He gripped the man's arm gratefully. "Thanks. Be careful you're not seen." Howie started away, still as scared as a cornered rabbit, and Cole had to say it. "You've got more guts than any other man in town."

He meant it and it was true. Howie looked at him with an expression that embarrassed him. He went scurrying down the stairs.

Cole turned and went back to his room, praying that Howie would not be seen by anyone who would tell Welch. If he was, he would soon be the third dead man in Coyote Springs.

He had suspected it all along, but now he knew for sure. Tod Welch had turned the expedition to the Indian camp from a brutal prank into a bloody massacre. By firing the first shot, by making the others think they were in real danger, he had triggered the mob psychology without which the thing couldn't have happened at all.

He closed the door to his room and crossed to the window, watching for Howie to cross the street to the saloon, thinking that Welch, while he must have cut the telegraph wires, must now be back at the saloon, or Howie could not have left.

He waited, and waited, growing more and more afraid for Howie's life. Finally, he saw Howie cross the street away down past the livery barn and telegraph office and disappear. He would enter the saloon by the back door, and his absence might go unobserved.

Cole stuffed the paper Howie had signed down into his revolver holster and jammed the gun down on top of it. He had enough, now, to arrest Welch and lodge him in jail. But there was no use doing it unless the sheriff agreed to keep him there.

Putting on his hat, he went out of his room, not even

bothering to lock the door this time. He went down the stairs and crossed the lobby to the door.

He headed down the street toward the jail, feeling like a target as he walked along the street, despite the fact that it was broad daylight. He knew that if Welch had killed both Easterling and Salgado, he wouldn't hesitate about killing him.

He'd get no help from Denver, and he'd get no help from anyone here in town. But maybe he could get the use of the jail. With that, he'd have a chance. Without it, it was just a matter of time until Welch or one of the others shot him in the back.

CHAPTER 15

Reed Sheridan, sitting in his office, saw the commotion begin in the street below, saw people begin hurrying, some running, toward the upper end of town. He went to the window and opened it. He listened to the shouts but was unable to make out what the commotion was about. Because of his closed windows and doors, and because of the distance, he had not heard the shotgun blast.

But he could guess what had happened. Someone else had been killed. Easterling's death had triggered this same kind of exodus from the main part of town.

But who? And by whom? the second question was more easily answered than the first. Welch. God damn him, it had to have been Welch.

Sheridan went back to his desk and sat down in his swivel chair. He realized suddenly and with some surprise that he hated Welch more than he had ever hated another human in his life.

He saw Welch in his mind, stocky, strong as a bull, bald-headed and red of face. He saw the wide mustache,

the blue eyes that were as hard and cold as ice. The surprising thing, he thought, was that Welch, being what he
was, hadn't killed before.

Yet, how did he know that? The man had come here
five or six years ago, bought the run-down Drovers Saloon,
fixed it up a little, and stayed. He had never talked about
the war or about his part in it. He had never even told anyone where he had come from or where he'd lived before
coming to Coyote Springs. And Welch wasn't the kind
you questioned about his past.

Welch, he remembered, had fired the first shot out at the
Indian camp. He'd shot down the old man with the empty
rifle, the rifle that hadn't even been raised or aimed, because the old Indian had known how empty it was.

That first shot, by Welch, had made them all begin
shooting. Sheridan frowned, trying to figure out why that
single shot had made them all begin firing at everything
that moved.

Mass hysteria, he thought. The same mass hysteria that
had made his own panic at Gettysburg trigger panic in everyone else along the line.

He realized that he could think about that now without
shame, without the self-revulsion that had always previously accompanied his memory of it. Now he knew that
there was no shame in being afraid. He knew that there
was not even overwhelming shame in running away and
that many a man who ran from his first fight ended up
making a fine soldier who later did his duty with pride and
dignity and even, sometimes, managed to die that way.

He also realized with a start, that Welch, by killing
those who had been with him at the Indian camp, was pro-

tecting himself, and that Welch would kill him, too, the instant he believed him to be a threat. What could he do?

Frowning faintly, he paced back and forth in his office. The street below was all but empty now. There were shouts and voices in the distance, which made a murmur in the still fall air. None of it was distinguishable.

Did Frank Cole, the United States marshal, have all the evidence he needed? Did he still have the photographs of the victims? By now, he no doubt had the names of all the participants.

At the last meeting, Welch's solution to the problem was to kill the man. But that was no answer and solved nothing for anyone. Other marshals would be sent to probe Cole's death. Someone could be made to talk. You couldn't make a whole town stay silent about a series of crimes, and it was foolish to think you could.

When the truth was known. . . . He thought of his family and of how hard he had worked to get his law degree and get to the position in life he now occupied. He would, no doubt, pay the same penalty that Tod Welch did. It would probably not be hanging but it would certainly be a term in prison, even if not more than a year or two. After all, the Custer massacre had occurred less than four months ago. Juries weren't likely to be too hard on whites who killed Indians. Particularly not a jury selected from Maxwell County residents.

But prison—for a lawyer—was worse than it was for most. He would be disbarred and would no longer be able to practice his profession. But there was a way. . . .

He considered it carefully. In a sense, it amounted to running away again, only this time he was going to care-

fully consider all the consequences before he did. He was
not going to panic and run. He was going to think it out.

He had friends among those who had helped massacre
the Indians: Art Ohlman. Pete Olivera. He liked Pat
Mosely, even if he didn't know him well and felt sorry
about Mosely's drinking and loss of his job, because he
sensed the torment in Mosely that had made him turn to
liquor to try to drown the guilt he felt over what had been
done. He even liked Howie Bracken, harmless and simple
Howie, who helped Welch in the saloon.

He didn't want to hurt anyone. But the truth was, the
thing he was considering wasn't going to hurt anyone. Except maybe Welch.

He stopped pacing suddenly and stared down into the
street. A man came running along it, headed for Norman
Reeves's Furniture Store and Undertaking Parlor. The
man saw Reed looking down from his window and yelled,
"Salgado's been killed! Someone blasted him in the chest
with a shotgun! He was getting ready to leave town!"

Whatever doubt remained in Sheridan's mind suddenly
disappeared. Marcus Easterling had been killed because he
refused to attend a conspirators' meeting in the back of
Brundage's store. Salgado had been killed because he was
getting ready to leave town, because, while he had not
been along on the Indian-camp raid, he had known everyone who had. Not that there weren't plenty of others in
town who also did.

Better, then, for everyone to go to prison, if that was
what it amounted to, than to be gunned down one by one
by a crazed and sadistic Welch. His mind made up, he now
only had to decide when it would be safest to try seeing

U. S. Marshal Cole. He would make a deal with the man.
Immunity in exchange for all the details of what had happened that awful day.

Was it running in the face of the enemy again? No, he
didn't think it was. Besides, he had settled the matter of
whether he was a coward or not during the ride out to the
Indian camp. He had decided that he was not.

He had shot one of the Indian men out there. Or he
thought he had. The man had gone down immediately
after he had fired at him. Of course it was possible he had
missed and that someone else had actually shot the man.
Unexpectedly, he thought of the way they worked a firing
squad: One man's rifle was always loaded with blanks.
That was supposed to let each man think he might not
have fired the fatal shot.

He saw Frank Cole come walking down the street with
Nora McKissick. Neither was talking to the other. They
walked solemnly to Nora's restaurant, where she left him
and disappeared inside. Cole continued on to the Western
Union office, just below the livery stable. Sending a telegram for help, thought Sheridan.

Standing there at the window, he saw Tod Welch gallop
down the alley to the rear of the saloon. Horse and rider
quickly disappeared. A little later, Howie Bracken came
from behind the saloon, hurried down the alley, and
crossed the intersection to disappear behind the hotel.
Hardly had he disappeared before the marshal came out of
the telegraph office. He had hardly been in the telegraph
office long enough to send a telegram, Sheridan thought,
let alone receive a reply to it. Where had Welch been and
why had he returned in such a hurry?

He didn't know, of course, but he could guess. Welch must have suspected Cole might telegraph Denver for help after the Salgado killing. He'd probably ridden out and cut the wires. Welch didn't much like to ride and wouldn't do it without good reason.

Sheridan wondered whether Cole had managed to get his telegram sent before the wires were cut.

He waited awhile, still indecisive. Then he saw Howie cross the street again, this time down below the livery stable, and again disappear.

Now was as good a time as any, he thought. He put on his hat, closed and locked his office door, and went down the outside stairway to the street. But instead of heading straight across to the hotel, he went down the side street, heading for the rear, intending to go in the back door and up the back stairs to eliminate any chance of being seen.

What he did not consider was that Tod Welch's view from the saloon was nearly as good as his had been from his office catercorner across from the Colorado Hotel.

Nor did he stop to think that, with Howie again inside the saloon, Welch wasn't pinned down behind the bar.

Casually, and almost indolently, he crossed the street and disappeared behind the hotel. He didn't see Welch come bursting from the front doors of the saloon. He didn't see him cross the street at a lumbering run.

He came to the alley behind the hotel and turned into it. And came face-to-face with a hard-breathing, red-faced Tod Welch.

He halted abruptly, trying to keep from looking as guilty as he felt, failing miserably. Welch asked, "Where you headed, Sheridan?"

Sheridan groped for words. None came. There was no logical destination for him down this dirt alleyway. Lamely, he finally got out, "A walk. Just a walk."

"Hear what happened to Juan Salgado? Just for trying to leave town?"

Sheridan felt the clutch of fear inside his chest. "I heard. But I'm not walking out of town."

"Going up the back stairs of the hotel, maybe? To see that U.S. marshal there?"

Sheridan shook his head. "Why should I do that? I'm in this thing just as deep as you."

"You sure as hell are. And you'd better remember it. I'd give up that walk if I was you."

Sheridan started to protest. Then he changed his mind. Welch knew where he had been headed. The pretense of taking a walk hadn't fooled him a bit.

Right now, Welch had no gun. But later on tonight . . . Sheridan knew suddenly that he was in greater danger than he had ever been before, even at Gettysburg, where two out of ten in the Union Army had been hit.

With a faint shrug, he turned and went back in the direction from which he had come. At the intersection, he turned his head and saw Frank Cole headed for the sheriff's office and jail. As soon as Cole disappeared inside, he saw Tod Welch cross the street and go into the saloon.

He climbed the stairs to his office. There was a small pistol in his desk, a double-barreled derringer. It was loaded, and caps were on both nipples. He stuck it down into the side pocket of his coat.

He left his office then and headed up the street toward home. Welch would have to try killing him tonight, he thought, and he'd better be ready for the man. He realized with prideful surprise that he wasn't terrified. He was scared and he might stay that way, but he was going to function. He wasn't going to run.

CHAPTER 16

Arthur Ohlman was in the barbershop when the shot was fired into Juan Salgado's chest. He heard it in the back part of his mind, but until he saw people hurrying up the street, he didn't realize what it had been.

He was shaving a customer, a cowboy from out of town. He finished, accepted the man's money, and then followed him out the door. He locked it and hurried uptown to see what had happened and to whom.

He didn't get as far as Salgado's house. Someone came running past and yelled breathlessly at him, "It's Salgado. Someone let him have it in the chest with a scatter-gun."

Ohlman stopped. He felt the touch of fear, because this was the second killing today.

Ohlman hesitated a moment there on the street. He didn't want to go back to his shop. He didn't feel like talking to anyone. Like Reed Sheridan, he knew who had killed both Easterling and Salgado. He also knew he was in danger himself, or would be the instant Welch thought that he might talk.

There was no danger of that, though, and Welch was probably aware of it. Ohlman was the one who had emptied his gun into the woman with the baby in the rickety lean-to. If he was brought to trial, he would pay as heavy a penalty as would Welch, because most of the others had seen what he had done.

He glanced toward home, then back toward the barbershop. He really didn't want to go to either place, but he had to go somewhere. He headed up the street.

Reaching his house, he went inside. His wife looked at him, looked away, then glanced quickly back. She asked, "What's the matter with you? You sick?"

He shook his head. He wanted a drink, but he knew if he got one at this time of day his wife would be full of questions and would make a big thing of it. So instead he got a cup of strong coffee from the pot simmering on the back of the stove. He didn't want his wife's company, but neither, suddenly, did he want to be alone. He sat down at the kitchen table, the coffee in front of him.

His wife continued her work in the kitchen for a while, occasionally glancing toward him. Finally she asked, "What's the matter with you if you're not sick?"

"Upset, I guess. Easterling murdered this morning, Juan Salgado just a little while ago."

"Salgado?" The surprise in her voice told him she hadn't heard. She was silent a moment, studying him closely, and finally she said, "It's that business out at the Indian camp, isn't it? Both of them were in on it, weren't they?"

"Salgado wasn't. He never showed up. Said his horse was lame." He stopped, realizing with a shock that he had just exposed to her his own involvement in the incident.

Hands on hips, she stared at him. Uncharacteristically and with genuine surprise, she said, "Well, I'll be damned. *You* were in on that, weren't you?"

"I didn't say that." But he would not look up and meet her glance.

The realization that he had been at the Indian camp seemed to have silenced her. Finally she asked shrilly, "Did you kill any of them?"

"Why? What difference would it make to you?"

"If you did, then that marshal will be arresting you. You'll go to prison, and what do you think I'll do? I can't cut hair." Her voice kept getting shriller as she spoke.

He said, "I don't give a damn what you do. Starve or try to get a job in the Drovers Saloon." That thought suddenly struck him funny and he laughed, but there was a quality of hysteria in the laugh.

She shrilled, "You rabbit, where did you ever find the courage to go out to that Indian camp? Or the courage to shoot any of them?"

He could feel his anger rising, slowly, but recklessly too. There had been more strain on him since he'd shot the Indian woman than ever before in his life. His wife continued to shrill at him until finally he said harshly, "Shut up and get me some more coffee!"

"Get your own damn coffee! I'm not your . . ."

He raised his glance. Something she saw in it stopped her in midsentence. She stared at him an instant, then silently crossed the kitchen and got the coffeepot.

Ohlman was remembering the Indian woman, and the hysterical way he had emptied his gun into her. Because she had been screaming at him.

Why, though, he asked himself silently, had he taken his wife's shrill abuse all these years? Why? He had to be some kind of idiot to take it day after day. He stared at her as she crossed the kitchen with the coffeepot, trying to see in her something of the girl he had married. He couldn't see it, because it wasn't there. And yet it had been the memory of that girl that had kept him with her all this time. Maybe in the hope that she would change.

But she wouldn't change. What had changed was his perception of her. She had always been exactly what she was right now, even on the day he'd married her. Trouble was, when a man and woman are keeping company, they only show each other their best side. And sometimes you marry someone without knowing anything about her at all. Without really knowing *what* she is like.

She poured his cup full. He reached out for the cup.

It may have been deliberate or it may have been an accident. But suddenly the hot coffee from the pot was pouring directly onto his hand instead of into the cup.

All the pent-up anger, guilt, frustration in him blew like a charge of dynamite. He swept cup, coffee, and pot away and halfway across the room with a quick movement of his arm. His wife stepped back, startled.

His hand burned like fire, fueling the rage in him. He lurched to his feet, lunged across the room after her. She saw the raw fury in his eyes, knew instinctively how dangerous it was, and whirled to try to get away.

She was too late. His fist smashed into her face, sending her backward, crashing into the stove. Blood came from her mouth. Terror came into her eyes. She was seeing in Arthur Ohlman the same thing that the Indian woman had seen and, like the Indian woman, she now began to scream. He came after her, and she made it to hands and knees, crawled toward the door, was halfway to it before he reached her again.

His fist, hard-clenched, came down like a hammer blow on the back of her head, driving her head and her face into the floor. Her screaming turned to whimpering, but he was clear out of his mind by now, out of control—the way he had been at the Indian camp.

He yanked her to her feet as if she were a doll, ripping her dress half off in the doing. He slammed her against the wall and held her there with one hand while the other smashed repeatedly into her face, beating, beating, until there was finally nothing recognizable about her but the wild terror in her eyes, and even that was numbing as her consciousness slipped away.

Finally, worn out, he let go and let her slip to the floor. He stared down at her, feeling purged and weak, but guilty, too, as guilty as he'd felt at the Indian camp. He said hoarsely, "I'm going. I'm taking the horse and I'm going and I'm never coming back."

She didn't say anything, just stared up at him like a dumb, wounded animal. He turned and strode from the house. He went to the stable and, with hands that were bloody and trembling, saddled the horse and bridled him. The horse smelled the blood and was made nervous by it, but as soon as Ohlman's hands were no longer close to his nostrils, he calmed somewhat.

Ohlman had only a few dollars in his pocket. He had the clothes on his back, and he had the horse.

But he was free! Oh, God, he was free! He felt as if a

hundred-pound load had been lifted from his back. He looked up at the golden cottonwoods and at the sky, with a few puffy white clouds floating in it, and for the first time in years saw how beautiful it was.

He had forgotten the Indian camp. He had forgotten Welch and the United States marshal that was in town. Exhausted both emotionally and physically, he mounted his horse and rode, heading uptown, north.

Behind him, he heard a shout. He turned his head and saw Reed Sheridan coming toward him on foot half a block away.

The sight of Reed Sheridan brought it all back to him: the Indian camp, the deaths of Easterling and Salgado, the U.S. marshal and the reporter who were in town.

He halted his horse. Sheridan reached him, a little out of breath. He stared at Ohlman, at the blood splattered on the front of his shirt, on his face and hands. He saw the wildness in Ohlman's eyes and asked, "What the hell? What happened to you?"

"Got enough, finally. Beat the hell out of her. Leaving. Leaving for good."

Sheridan stared up at him. He said, "You can't. Welch will catch and kill you before you're ten miles out of town. He thought I was going to the marshal and he threatened me. And if you think he won't do it, go down and look at the bodies of Easterling and Salgado."

"I can't stay. I beat the hell out of her."

"Then at least stay until it gets dark. Go on up to my place. You can stay in the stable with your horse. I'll bring you some food and things."

Ohlman nodded numbly. What Sheridan was telling him made sense. The hysteria was leaving him and he was beginning to think again.

He turned his horse and rode toward Reed Sheridan's house. Sheridan turned and headed back toward his office, across the street from the hotel.

It was a long time after her husband left before Mrs. Ohlman moved. She was dazed and only partly conscious as she pushed herself to her feet, using the table to help. She stood there swaying a moment, looking down at her torn and bloodied dress, still filled with disbelief at what had happened to her. She had screamed at her husband before, and sometimes he'd fought back, with words. Sometimes he'd only got up and left. But never had he struck her, though she had sometimes seen the desire to in his eyes.

She staggered out of the kitchen, found a mirror, and stared into it. When she saw what he had done to her face, her own fury, always volatile anyway, rose within her. Damn him! He wasn't going to get away with this.

She staggered toward the front door. Unsteadily she stumbled outside, down the walk, and into the street. Silently, conserving her strength and breath, she hurried down the sunny, tree-lined street toward the center of town.

People stopped to stare at her. A buggy went around her, because she was in the middle of the street.

She made no sound. She ran out of breath and slowed to a walk. She passed the intersection where stood the Colorado Hotel and went on until she reached the stone-block jail, over which hung a weathered sign, MAXWELL COUNTY JAIL. She went inside.

The sheriff was sitting at his desk. Dave Thorne got up instantly, staring, for an instant not recognizing her. Then he shoved the chair at her and said, "Sit down, Mrs. Ohlman. Easy now. Get your breath, and then tell me what happened to you."

"It was him. My husband. He beat me. I want you to arrest him and put him in jail and throw away the key."

He got her a glass of water and brought it to her. Her mouth was so badly smashed she could hardly drink, but she managed to get a couple of small swallows down.

Less hysterically now, she said, "Find him. Arrest him and throw him into jail."

Thorne shook his head. The beating was a brutal one, but he knew, as most of the townspeople did, what this woman had put Art Ohlman through in the past few years.

She stared at him unbelievingly. "You won't?"

"I didn't say that," he said. "I'll go look for Art. You bring charges against him and I'll put him in jail. But it will be for only a few weeks."

"If you won't keep him in jail for beating me, then do it for his murdering Indians. He was in on that thing down at the Indian camp."

Thorne said, "All right. Maybe I can arrest him for that. Now go home, Mrs. Ohlman. Go home and go to bed. Get one of your friends to come in and take care of you."

She stared at him—bitter, black hatred in her eyes. Then, surprisingly without another word, she turned and left the jail. She slammed the door savagely as she went out.

Thorne suddenly wished he'd stayed the hell out of town, because now that he was back he was damned if he did and damned if he didn't. Arresting any of the killers of the Indians would end his career as sheriff here. Not arresting them would likely expose him to federal charges of complicity.

The murders of Easterling and Salgado were another kettle of fish, however. He had no evidence, but he knew within his heart that it had to be Welch. He didn't know what to do, except that whatever it was it had better be soon, before the whole town panicked and came apart at the seams.

And yet, despite his troubles, he couldn't help feeling satisfaction that Art Ohlman had finally done what he should have done years before. Maybe he needn't have done it so savagely, but, then, if he'd done it years before, he wouldn't have needed to.

CHAPTER 17

Helpless to send for deputies, Cole knew that if he did not capture Welch today, in daylight, there was a good chance he might not live out the night. He was a deadly threat to Welch, a threat of prison at the least, hanging at the worst now that Welch had killed twice here in town. But Welch would not be trying to kill him just because of that. He had humiliated Welch.

Furthermore, Cole knew better than to walk into the Drovers Saloon and try to take Welch out of it. That would be tempting fate. Those who had killed at the Indian camp had probably decided by now that one more killing could get them into no deeper trouble than the trouble they were already in.

The sheriff was the best, maybe the only, chance he had. He needed the use of the jail, so that he could pick the killers up one by one, put them in jail, and know that they were guarded while he went after the others.

Flagg had been busy all day, trying to interview sullen and reluctant townspeople. Right now he was going into the Drovers Saloon, probably to continue his interviews. Cole wondered how much he had really been able to glean from his interviews and how his story was coming along.

He continued along the street, feeling more exposed than he had in a long time. Glancing up and down, he saw the windows, the narrow passageways between buildings, the high false building fronts. Any of fifty places could conceal a hidden rifleman, and it would take only one shot.

He reached the jail and went inside. Thorne stared at him from his swivel chair with open hostility. "You sure brought a peck of trouble to this town when you came."

"The trouble was already here."

"You think Easterling and Salgado would have been killed if you hadn't come?"

Cole said, "Your reasoning puzzles me. If you'd done your job, there wouldn't have been any need for me to come."

"My job? My job isn't to protect a bunch of damned savages. If the men here hadn't killed them, they'd likely have killed some white ranchers before very long."

"What with? Rocks?"

Thorne got up angrily. "What the hell did you come in here for anyway? I told you I didn't intend to help. Killin' them Indians wasn't no worse than diggin' out a den of wolves."

Cole said, "There are charges I can bring against you. Charges that will stick in federal court. Accessory after the fact. Obstructing a federal officer. Complicity in the deaths of Easterling and Salgado. And if anyone else is killed, accessory and conspiracy. You know who killed Easterling and Salgado?"

"Who?"

"Welch."

"But you have no proof. I questioned everyone near the scenes of both murders, and no one saw a thing. There were no witnesses. Welch says he was at home, and I can't prove he wasn't. What do you want me to do? There's no proof."

"It was Welch. And if he isn't caught, he's going to kill again."

"Then, you go catch him. He's probably over there at the Drovers right now."

Cole said, "I wouldn't get three feet inside the door."

"Then, what do you want me to do? I'm between a rock and a hard place, mister. If it looks as if I helped you arrest the men who killed those Indians, I'm through here in Maxwell County. I'd never get elected again. And if I don't help you, you'll bring all them charges against me and I'll go to jail. You sure don't give a man much choice."

"I didn't come down here to give you a choice." Cole stared at him coldly for a moment.

"All right. I'll back you up the moment you have hard proof. I'll even hold your prisoners for you. Beyond that, you're on your own."

It was as much as Cole had expected to get, and, besides, he'd had tough assignments before. He nodded. "All right. But I warn you, if I arrest anybody and they get away . . ."

"They won't."

Cole stepped outside to the walk. He stared across at the Drovers Saloon. Maybe now would be the best time, he thought. But he knew it wouldn't. He'd had a run-in with

Welch in his saloon yesterday, a run-in that had almost come to gunplay. If Welch shot him down today, he could claim self-defense, and he might even get away with it. But whether he did or not would be irrelevant, because Cole would be dead.

Someone was suddenly propelled through the doors of the Drovers with enough force to send him staggering across the walk and make him collapse in the street. Cole recognized Flagg by his suit. He crossed the intersection at a run and was in time to help Flagg climb to his feet.

One of Flagg's eyes was swelling shut. His nose was bleeding profusely. One ear was bleeding, and there was a bruise the size of a walnut on one cheekbone. He was only half conscious, and whenever he moved, his face twisted with pain.

Cole glanced at the doors of the saloon. He could see faces peering over the swinging doors, and faces behind the dirty windows. He held Flagg upright as he asked, "Who did it? Who?"

Flagg just shook his head. He didn't seem able to talk. Every time he opened his mouth, blood dribbled out of it.

Flagg needed help, a lot of it. However much he might like to, Cole couldn't leave him there while he went inside to square accounts for the beating Flagg had received.

He said, "Come on. I'll get you to where you can be taken care of." He headed toward the hotel.

He heard light footsteps running behind him and, turning his head, saw Nora McKissick running after them. Her face was pale, her eyes shocked at the way Flagg looked. "Where are you taking him?"

"The hotel. Maybe I can get somebody. . . ."

"You bring him to my place."

"That's not going to make things any easier for you here in town."

"Let me worry about that." She positioned herself on the other side of Flagg, and together they half carried, half dragged him up the street. Flagg didn't even try to talk any more.

Cole tried to carry most of Flagg's weight, but it wasn't possible.

After turning the corner by the hotel, Cole stopped, saying, "Rest a minute."

They stopped. Cole glanced at Flagg. "Who did it?"

Flagg stared at him with glazed eyes. Cole repeated, "Who did it?"

"Bartender," Flagg managed to say.

Cole said, "Welch. He's the first one I'm going to have to get. I finally threatened the sheriff into letting me lodge prisoners in the jail."

They went on, stopping again to rest at the entrance of the alley leading toward Nora's house. There was no sign of life at the Salgado house. If only Salgado had realized how dangerous Welch was, he wouldn't have been making preparations to leave in broad daylight, Cole thought, but it was too late now.

They went on, and finally reached the back door of Nora McKissick's house. She held the door while Cole helped Flagg inside. He laid the newspaperman down on a couch in Nora's parlor.

Flagg's eyes were beginning to show a little more comprehension. Nora went after water and towels, and Cole asked, "Think you've got broken ribs?"

Flagg nodded. "Could. It sure hurts when I breathe."

Cole didn't say anything, waiting for Nora to return. Flagg said resentfully, talking thickly through bruised and battered lips, "I was just talking to people, and that bartender came from behind the bar and began beating me."

"Know who you were talking to?"

"When he beat me? A drunk cowboy named Mosely."

Cole said, "He was one of those who helped kill the Indians. In fact he was one that brought the news they were out there to town. He's been drinking like a fish ever since, so much so that he got fired from his job. Welch must have been afraid he'd talk."

Nora returned with a pan of water and some towels. Cole helped her as best he could to get Flagg's coat, vest, and shirt off. There were a couple of angry red places where Flagg's ribs were. He said, "He ought to be wrapped tightly to hold those ribs in place if they are cracked."

Nora nodded. Once, her glance met Cole's over Flagg's head. Her eyes were troubled. Having cleaned up Flagg's battered face as best she could and put pieces of court plaster where the skin was broken, she got a sheet, ripped it into strips, and then, with Cole's help, wrapped it around Flagg's torso tightly.

Cole knew he had to leave, and he didn't want to leave Flagg there, because if Welch thought he'd gotten anything out of Mosely he might come after him. He said, "I'll help him back to the hotel."

"I'm not going to open the restaurant tonight. I doubt if anyone would come in even if I did."

Cole said, "Thanks for helping him. I'd have tried, but I wouldn't have done nearly as well as you did."

She smiled wanly. "Please be careful. Welch will certainly be after you now."

He nodded. He helped Flagg out and down the path to the alley. Flagg was pretty well able to walk by himself by now. Cole said, "Stay in the hotel. You've got all the interviews you need, at least until I've got them all in jail."

Flagg nodded mutely, no argument left in him. Cole got him to the hotel, helped him in and up to his room. He lighted the lamp and told Flagg to lock his door. Flagg would be safe, at least as long as Cole remained alive.

The sun now was fully down, its dying rays staining the pile of clouds in the west a brilliant gold. Cole went out the back, then up the alley for a full block before he crossed over and reached the alley that ran behind the saloon. Welch was the first, the most important, the most dangerous. If he could get Welch in jail, arresting the others might be possible. However he tried not to, he could not help looking back over his shoulder, and his ears were turned to each small sound. Twice he nearly dived for the shelter of a nearby stable, hearing a slight scuffing noise each time. Both times, the noise turned out to have been made by dogs, which immediately began to bark at him.

The gold faded from the clouds, and the whole sky turned gray. This, he realized, was the most dangerous time of day for him. Welch and the others could see to shoot, but they could hide in the shadows and avoid being seen themselves.

He reached the intersection of the block in which the Drovers Saloon was. He entered the alley beyond.

The shot came from almost immediately ahead, and he never even saw the rifleman. All he saw was the muzzle flash, and he felt a blow in his thigh, a blow so hard that it took the leg out from under him and dumped him into the alley dust. A second shot followed close on the heels of the first, but because he had fallen, this bullet whistled harmlessly overhead.

Cole, his leg numb, rolled frantically across the alley toward the doubtful shelter of a broken-down picket fence. Rolling, he yanked his revolver from its holster, thumbing back the hammer as he did. Lying still, he waited for the third muzzle flash and for something at which to shoot.

It never came. He heard retreating footsteps that finally faded to nothingness. He lay still for several moments more, feeling the warm wetness as blood from his wound soaked his pants and the dust beneath.

Nothing moved except for the three dogs that had been following him and now barked excitedly, their hackles up. Cole waited until it was almost completely dark in the alley, then ripped a board from the fence to use as a cane and pushed himself to his feet. He took just an instant to make sure the signed paper was still in the bottom of his holster; then, gun in one hand, cane in the other, he limped back up the alley in the direction of Nora McKissick's house.

It was too dark to tell how bad his wound was, but the pain was beginning, and it made things reel before his eyes.

He was nearly helpless now, and they could have followed and killed him easily. But they didn't come. He made it to the stable behind Nora's house, and she met him there, having heard the shots. She helped him into the house but was cautious enough to draw all the shades before she knelt to look at the wound in his leg.

CHAPTER 18

Blood had run down his leg, filled his boot, and soaked his pants leg, which had two holes in it. With trembling hands and a deathly pale face, Nora got a kitchen knife and slit his pants and underwear from his boot top to well above the knee. She asked, "How about the boot? Do you think you can stand it if I try to pull it off?"

He said, "Try. There's blood in it, so it ought to come off easily." His head was whirling and he felt dizzy enough to fall off the kitchen chair. Blood had dripped onto the floor, and he regretted dirtying up her house. He started to apologize, but right then she began trying to ease off the boot and he gripped the sides of the chair and clenched his teeth to keep from crying out.

The boot came off, and now Nora peeled his slit pants leg and underwear up and looked at the wound.

The hole made by the bullet's entry was small, blue around the edges, and just oozing blood. Where the bullet had exited, the hole was several times as large and the flesh was shredded. But the blood did not come in spurts and no bone fragments were visible. Cole thought, "Thank God for that!"

Having examined the wound, Nora now hurried around, getting whiskey for disinfecting, towels for compresses, the remainder of the sheet she had used to bandage Flagg's broken ribs. Cole said, "I'm sorry."

"For what?"

"For bringing all this mess and trouble to you."

She paused, hands on hips, and stared at him. "Who else would you take it to?" She got a dishpan, placed it beneath his leg, then said, "This will hurt," and poured whiskey over the raw and bleeding wound.

It was as if someone had laid a red-hot iron against his leg. Cole hung onto the chair, head whirling, while Nora watched him and once reached up to steady him. She made a compress then, of a small, clean towel, and laid it over the exit wound. "It probably ought to be sewed up, but I don't know how to do that and there's no doctor, only a veterinarian, in town. You'll have an awful scar."

"Never mind the scar. I don't go around much without my pants." He tried to grin at his feeble joke, but it didn't quite come off.

Nora finished bandaging. "I don't suppose you'd consider lying down for a while?"

"I'll sit for a while. But I can't quit. They've beaten Flagg and shot me, and if I don't get Welch in jail tonight neither one of us has got the chance of a snowball in hell."

"Could you eat anything?" She was busy wiping up the floor. When she had finished, she carried the dishpan filled with bloody water outside and emptied it. When she came back, he said, "I suppose I ought to try. Give me that whiskey bottle first and I'll put a little of it inside of me."

She poured him half a glass of it, then crossed to the stove and began to build a fire. He watched her, dizzy, half in and half out of it, but not so much so that he couldn't appreciate watching her. Once, she turned her head, caught his glance, and flushed. She said, "You'll make it if you can look at me like that."

Cole said, "This is pretty quick, but when somebody is trying to kill you, things have to move pretty quick. I want you to marry me."

She stared at him in astonishment. "I've only known you a couple of days."

"I'm not going to be here more than a couple more. And by helping me, you've practically made it impossible for you to stay here after I am gone."

"That's not enough reason to marry you."

He suddenly was scared. He wasn't used to saying the things he knew needed to be said, and he wasn't sure if he could do it right. He said, "I've never been married. I've never known a woman I wanted to marry. But I want to marry you. I want to spend the rest of my life with you."

"I can't give you an answer now. I've got to think."

He nodded. He said, "I'd be very good to you."

She bent, kissed him lightly on the cheek. "I know you would," and went on past him to the stove.

Cole got to his feet, tried putting his weight on the wounded leg, and discovered that he could. He hobbled around the kitchen while Nora fixed him some scrambled eggs. He discovered that the more he walked on the wounded leg, the better he was able to.

Pain came and went in throbbing waves. He sat down again and watched Nora work. After several more minutes she put a plate on the table for him, scrambled eggs, warmed bread, milk. He got up, moved to the table, and sat down. She sat across from him, watching his face. Now and then he glanced up, met her eyes, and knew she was considering his proposal, weighing it, trying to decide. He reached across and took her hand, feeling her decision was very close, and after another moment she nodded her head, a certain brightness in her eyes. She said, "All right. I will marry you and go away with you. But for God's sake be careful now."

He squeezed her hand, for the moment overwhelmed, and said, "We don't know each other very well, but I believe we know what we need to know. And I *will* be careful."

"Can't you telegraph for help?"

"I tried. The lines have been cut."

"Then they do intend to try and murder you. And Mr. Flagg as well."

"Yes. They will try. But that isn't as easy as it may sound. I was through the war. I have been a law officer ever since."

She nodded, biting her lip, determined not to beg him not to do his job, because she knew it would do no good. He finished eating and got to his feet. He checked the loads in his gun, unable in this instant to remember whether he had fired a while ago or not. He said, "I've got to go. Leave the lamps here and the shades drawn and lock the back door and the front one too after I've gone out."

She nodded. He drew her to him, this being the first time, bent his head, and kissed her on the mouth. It was a lingering kiss, and when she drew away, her eyes had filled with tears. She knew how little chance he had and didn't really believe she would ever see him again.

He released her and limped through the house to the front door. He went out as silently as he could, leaving her to close and lock it behind him. Then he was out in the early-autumn darkness, with a breeze rustling the yellow cottonwood leaves over his head and no other sound except for the distant barking of a dog.

He stood on the porch for an instant, getting his eyes accustomed to near darkness, to the faint light that came from the stars.

Carefully, testing each step, he crossed the porch and stepped down onto the path. They would be watching this house, but maybe they were watching the rear, expecting him to come out there. There was a chance he'd get away.

He drew his gun in the shadow of a huge lilac bush, thumbed back the hammer. It made a slight click and he froze an instant, but no sound came and nothing happened, so he went on, moving away uptown instead of down.

Even though a limited number of men might be hunting him with guns, he knew that as long as the whole town was solidly against him he had no chance to win. No one would warn him or help him. Not all of them had participated in the Indian killings or even approved of them, but all of them knew what the exposure of the killings meant to the future of the town. Besides that, there were close and small-town loyalties. Of all the people in this town, only one had been outraged enough about the Indians' deaths to write to the marshal's office in Denver to protest.

He could use the help of Cliff Tolliver now, but going for his help would put Tolliver in too much danger. He thought of Brundage, who could, if he would, muster some support among the townspeople for him and perhaps make it possible for him to make his arrests and survive. His persuasion would have to be that a few men killing a few Indians is bad enough, but a whole town co-operating to conceal the killings by consenting to the murder of a U.S. marshal and a newspaper reporter would mean the end of the town and its ultimate abandonment. He had a feeling that Brundage was more heavily involved financially in Coyote Springs than anyone, and he figured that explained Brundage's throwing in with the killers in trying to conceal their crimes.

He knew where Brundage's store was, but he didn't know where he lived. All he needed to do, however, was to locate the largest, most elaborate house in town. There, he felt sure, he would find Brundage.

A hundred yards away from Nora McKissick's house, he was satisfied that he had not been observed or followed. He began to move more freely and more swiftly, now and then stopping and concealing himself as he spotted someone on a porch or in a yard or just walking along the street.

He cursed his lack of knowledge of the town, because his leg pained him fiercely, but he kept going, and at last, near the upper edge of town, he spotted a three-story house with gables and scrollwork eaves and a meticulously kept picket fence and lawn.

He stepped over the fence to avoid a possible squeak in the gate. There were lamps burning in the house. He held his breath, hoping no dog would rush at him and bark, and peered into the window at the front of the house.

Brundage was there. He had guessed correctly that Brundage would own the most elaborate house in town. He limped to the front porch, crossed it silently, and then twisted the bell on the door.

Brundage opened it. Cole already had the screen door open, and he pushed his way inside and closed the door behind him. Brundage's face showed both surprise and anger until Cole said, "Sorry about pushing in that way. But I was shot a while ago and I don't want to get shot again."

"What are you doing here?"

"I figure you're the man with the most influence in this town. I figure if you think on it for a minute you'll decide you don't really want a U.S. marshal and a *News* reporter murdered here. What happened at that Indian camp is bad enough. What happened to Mr. Easterling and Mr. Salgado is just as bad. But if you let it continue, there won't be anything left of this town in a couple of years."

"What do you think I can do? I wasn't in on that business down at the Indian camp, and I didn't kill either Easterling or Salgado."

"You were at the Indian camp, supervising the cleanup there."

"You followed us?"

"And I saw every face."

"I still don't know what I can do."

"You can call a town meeting. You can convince these people that the five remaining men who killed those Indians aren't worth any more people getting killed."

Brundage said, "It won't do any good."

"It won't do any harm."

"Welch will. . . ."

"Kill you? What makes you think he won't anyway? Welch is a mad dog."

Brundage considered that. So far, Welch had done what Brundage told him to, but that didn't mean he always would. He nodded. "All right. I'll call a town meeting first thing tomorrow."

"Tomorrow won't do. It's got to be tonight."

Brundage hesitated. Cole could see that he was afraid. Of Welch, probably. Afraid Welch would come after him the instant he showed signs of wavering. Welch would certainly consider calling a town meeting wavering.

Cole said, "I'm going to get out of this, one way or another. And when I do, I'm going to see that you're brought to trial as an accessory. Unless you help me now."

Brundage nodded. "All right. I'll go down and ring the church bell right away."

Cole nodded. He went back out the door and, moving as cautiously as he had before, headed downtown toward the Drovers Saloon.

CHAPTER 19

It was Welch who had shot Cole, but, failing to kill him and knowing Cole was not only armed but probably a crack shot, he had hastily withdrawn. But only far enough so that Cole would think he had gone. He kept Cole in sight, saw him get to his feet and limp painfully toward Nora McKissick's house. If there had been more light, he might have tried again, but there wasn't sufficient light to see his sights.

He saw Cole go into Nora McKissick's house, saw her draw the blinds, saw the light increase as she lighted another lamp. He waited.

He waited a long time. He knew he had scored a solid hit on Cole. He also knew it was unlikely that he had broken the bone in Cole's leg with his bullet. If he had, Cole wouldn't have been able to walk at all, even with the help of a fence picket to use as a cane. There was a good possibility, however, that Cole had lost so much blood that he'd be out of action for tonight.

After about three quarters of an hour, Welch decided he

would wait no more. By now, Cole was probably unconscious or asleep. What better time to be rid of him with no
risk to himself?

He crossed the back porch of Nora's house carefully,
testing each step in case the boards might squeak. He
reached the back door and opened the screen. Carefully, he
tried the doorknob, not surprised that the door was locked.

He stepped back, as far as he could without letting go of
the screeen. Then, with all his considerable strength, he
rushed the door, hitting it, on the side where the lock was,
with a powerful shoulder. The door burst open and Welch
staggered across the room to crash against the wall on the
far side of it.

His gun was in his hand. Now he cocked it and looked
around for Cole.

Nora McKissick stood beside the stove, staring at him
with startled and frightened eyes. Welch growled,
"Where is the son of a bitch?"

"He's gone. He went out the front door ten minutes
ago."

He crossed to her. He seized a handful of hair. "Don't
lie to me!"

She was frightened, but her glance met his steadily.
"Look around. See for yourself."

Still holding her by the hair, his gun in the other hand,
he said, "Pick up one of those lamps. We'll look together."

She obeyed. Holding her in front of him, pulling
sufficiently on her hair to make her face contort with pain,
he pushed her through the door into the dining room and
into the parlor, beyond. Cole wasn't there and there was no
place he could hide. He said, "All right, now the bed-

rooms. And be quiet. If you yell, I'll put the first bullet into you." He figured if Cole was unconscious or asleep it would be in one of the two bedrooms.

But they were empty too and so were the closets. Welch released Nora. He didn't bother to threaten her. He just gave her a shove and went back out the kitchen door. Knowing that Cole was somewhere out in the darkness, he still doubted if Cole would have remained in hiding while he was in the house with Nora. He moved carefully away down the alley toward the rear door of the Drovers Saloon.

A padlock was on it. He unlocked it and went inside, then dropped the bar into place. He didn't want Cole coming in this way, surprising him. He shoved the revolver down into his belt as he entered the saloon proper, thinking that if he'd had the shotgun with which he'd killed Salgado a while ago, Cole would now be dead.

Mosely was sitting at a table in the corner, his head down on his arms. Olivera was sitting in a penny-ante poker game. Bracken was tending bar. Sheridan and Ohlman, being friends, were probably together either at Ohlman's house or at Sheridan's. Both of them were losing their grip, but he could take care of them after he'd gotten rid of the marshal and Flagg.

He crossed the room and shook Mosely. "Come on out back, Pat. I want to talk to you."

Mosely peered at him with bloodshot eyes. Welch knew he was drunk, but he didn't think he was drunk enough to be incapacitated. He went to Olivera next. He said, "Play out the hand, Pete, and then come out back. I want to talk to you."

Olivera nodded. He was the steadiest of the whole bunch, Welch thought. But he didn't really know how much he could get out of Mosely. The man hadn't said anything and hadn't shown any signs of cracking up. Except for the drinking, which was unusual for him.

He watched Pat Mosely get up and stagger into the back room. He got his shotgun, the new one, from underneath the bar, and followed him. Pat sat down on a whiskey cask and stared at the floor between his knees. After a few minutes Olivera came in, and Welch closed and barred the door leading to the saloon. He said bluntly, "I tried to kill him a while ago but I only got him in the leg. He's still alive, and as long as he is, he's dangerous."

Olivera asked, "What about Sheridan and Ohlman? Where are they?"

"Coming apart, like Easterling and Salgado did."

Olivera was watching him closely. Mosely seemed to have sobered up considerably. Olivera asked, "You going to kill them like you did Easterling and Salgado?"

"Maybe. But the marshal's first."

Mosely spoke for the first time. "And what about us? You going to kill us too?"

"Not unless I think you're going to spill something."

Olivera said, "You want something from us. What is it? You want us to help you kill the marshal and that reporter, Flagg?"

"That's exactly what I want."

Outside, faintly, the church bell began to ring. Welch didn't need to be told why it rang. It was the middle of the week and there were no church services tonight. Brundage was having it rung to call a town meeting. Probably because Cole had forced him to.

A town meeting might mean the townspeople would switch sides. They might decide to help the marshal out. If they did, then the sheriff would also get over on the other side.

He said, "Brundage is probably having that rung to call a town meeting. So if we're going to get Cole and Flagg, we'd better do it now."

"What do you want us to do?"

Welch looked at Olivera. "You go to the hotel and get that reporter. Bring him to Nora McKissick's house. Bring him out the back door of the hotel, and if he tries to yell, stuff something in his mouth."

"Why Nora's house?"

"Because that marshal's sweet on her. If he thinks she's in danger, he'll come running."

Olivera nodded. He went out into the saloon, closing the door behind him. Mosely looked at Welch apprehensively. "What do you want me to do?"

"Go up to Nora's house right now. Hide yourself someplace where you can see the front door. Get yourself a rifle, and if the marshal tries to go inside, blow his damn head off. I don't want to risk him getting back in there before we do."

"Where are you going to be?"

"At the back door with this scatter-gun. As soon as Olivera gets back with the reporter, we'll all go inside."

"How do you expect to get word to Cole?"

"I'll leave word with Howie. Sooner or later, when he don't find me anyplace else, Cole will come in here looking for me."

Mosely said, "It'll take me a few minutes to get my rifle. It's down at the stable, in my saddle boot."

Welch said, "All right. But don't try running out on me. You know what happened to Easterling and Salgado. Don't think the same thing can't happen to you, no matter how far you ride."

Mosely nodded. "I won't run out. I'll be up at Nora's house in ten minutes at the most." He, too, went out through the saloon.

Welch leaned his shotgun against the back door. He went into the saloon and spoke to Howie behind the bar. "That marshal, Cole, will be in here looking for me after a while. Tell him we're up at Nora McKissick's house. Tell him we've got Nora and we'll kill her if he don't give himself up. And tell him to bring those photographs."

Howie's eyes looked scared, but he nodded. Welch returned to the back room and left by the back door, taking his shotgun, padlocking the door behind him.

It suddenly struck him as strange that he had never doubted Howie Bracken's loyalty. Hell, Howie had stopped at the edge of the Indian camp. And Howie was really a rabbit underneath. Howie might even be the one who had notified the marshal's office in Denver about the Indian camp. Except, he thought, that Howie couldn't write.

He hurried along the alley, his revolver in his belt, the double-barreled shotgun in his hands with both hammers cocked. He was, perhaps, more alert than he had ever been in his life.

As he walked and his eyes searched the darkness ahead of him, a part of his mind considered the contradiction in men when it came to killing. Most of them considered hunting fun. Few of them would hesitate to kill a hog or butcher a steer. What was so different about a man?

A further contradiction was that most of the men who had gone to the Indian camp hadn't hesitated about killing Indians. But the killing of Easterling and Salgado had frightened them. Maybe, though, that had been because it had made them fear for themselves.

The real trouble with killing wasn't the moral aspects of it. The real trouble was that the need for it kept growing. Like this Indian business. It hadn't stopped with the Indians. Easterling had had to be killed and so had Salgado. Now Cole and Flagg had to be killed, and after that probably Sheridan and Ohlman. And certainly Tolliver, who was most likely the one who had written the marshal's office to begin with.

And then more marshals would show up. Welch suddenly made up his mind that as soon as Cole and Flagg were dead, he was going to take what he had and leave. Even if he had to just abandon the saloon. Because if he stayed, more and more and more of the people in town were going to crack. With each killing, someone would get more scared. No. It was too dangerous to stay. But he needed time. He needed a couple of weeks, and he wouldn't get it as long as either Cole or Flagg was alive.

He reached Nora McKissick's house. He stationed himself at the corner of the stable and crouched where he could plainly see and was in shotgun range of the back door. The gun was loaded with buckshot. If Cole came to that door, he was dead.

He had waited only five minutes when he saw Mosely come into sight at the side of the house. Mosely waved to let him know he was in position, and then he disappeared.

Nothing happened. A cricket began to chirp in the stable. A breeze stirred the leaves of the cottonwoods.

It seemed like a long time, but it could not have been very long. Welch heard a scuffing in the alley. Thinking it might be Cole hobbling along, he eased back to the fence, shotgun in front of him, ready to fire instantly.

The scuffing grew louder. Welch raised the gun to his shoulder, pointing as he would if he were duck hunting, since he was unable to see the front sight.

Two shapes came dimly into view instead of one, and Welch lowered the gun. The shapes came closer, and a few moments later, Olivera came through the gate, half carrying, half dragging the reporter, Flagg.

There was no mistaking the fear that showed in Flagg's eyes when he saw Welch. Welch said, "I'll go in first. You bring him in and then go out front and get Pat. Then all we've got to do is wait."

He tiptoed across the porch and opened the screen door. There was no longer any way for Nora to lock the back door, so it stood slightly ajar. Since he didn't know whether she possessed a firearm or not, Welch took no chances and burst in, much as he had before.

She was washing dishes at the sink. She turned her head to look at him, more anger than fear in her this time. "What do you want now?"

Welch didn't answer her. He turned and stuck his head out the door. "All right. Bring him in."

Olivera came in, dragging Flagg behind. He pushed Flagg into a chair, then went back out. A moment later, he came in again, this time followed by Mosely, who, while his eyes were red, seemed completely sober now.

Welch said, "Olivera, go into the parlor and keep watch

in there. Keep your gun in your hand and no lights, not even a match to light a smoke. That marshal is dangerous."

Olivera disappeared through the door leading to the dining room. Welch said, "Pat, go out and cut some clothesline. Make it fast."

Mosely went out. He was back in an instant, a coil of clothesline in his hand. Welch pulled Flagg's hands behind him and tied him so tightly that Flagg grunted with the pain. Finished with that, he knelt and tied Flagg's feet. He looked at Nora. "All right. You're next."

For an instant her expression looked as though she meant to resist. Deciding it was useless, she sat down obediently in a straight-backed chair and passively let Welch tie her hands and feet.

Welch pointed to one side of the kitchen door, over by the stove. "Pat, you settle yourself over there."

Mosely obeyed. Welch took up a position on the other side of the back door, which still stood slightly ajar. He didn't see how they could fail. Cole was all alone. There wasn't a chance he'd gotten any help this soon, even if Brundage was trying to persuade the townspeople to help. And the sheriff wasn't going to help. He'd already made that clear. So he waited, his ears tuned for the slightest sound, his glance fixed on the back door, which moved slightly back and forth in the evening breeze.

CHAPTER 20

As soon as he left Brundage's house, Cole headed for the saloon. He had lost the fence picket, so he tore another off a nearby fence to use as a cane. Putting part of his weight on the fence picket saved him considerable pain in his wounded leg, but he was getting weaker steadily. He had lost a lot of blood and he was still losing it. The towel compress Nora had put on his leg was soaked. So were the bandages she had wound around the compress to keep it in place.

His slit pants leg and underwear flapped in the evening breeze as he walked. He knew his strength wouldn't last much longer, so he had to try taking Welch while he still had enough of it left to cope with him.

Knowing that Welch might be stalking him, just as he was stalking Welch, he tried staying in shadows as much as possible, and he kept his gun in his hand, the hammer back.

It was still early and there were lights in the windows of many of the stores below the Colorado Hotel. Light came from the windows and swinging doors of the Drovers Saloon. Risky as it was, Cole knew he no longer had a choice. He had to burst into the Drovers and try taking Welch in there. But unless he had the advantage of surprise, he was dead.

He therefore angled through a vacant lot and approached the Drovers from the rear. He checked the back door, saw the padlock on it, and then sidled along the building toward the front.

He didn't dare risk being seen peering into the window. He'd just have to burst through the doors, take Welch first, and then, if there were others in there gunning for him, do the best he could with them.

A spasm of nausea, caused by the pain and loss of blood, ran over him. He waited until it had passed. Then, moving as fast as his wounded leg and the fence picket would permit, he shoved through the swinging doors, gun raised and ready, hammer cocked.

Howie Bracken was behind the bar, suddenly looking very scared. Others in the saloon turned their heads curiously. But there was no Welch. There were no others waiting to gun him down.

He stepped aside so that he wouldn't make a target for anyone outside. He spoke to Howie across the suddenly silent room. "Where is he?"

"He left a message for you. Said he'd be up at Nora McKissick's house. Said he'd kill her if you didn't come give yourself up. And he said to bring the photographs."

Cole had peaked his nerves for the showdown here in the saloon; the letdown left him feeling weak. So did the knowledge that Welch had Nora and that he would do exactly what he said he would.

He studied Howie Bracken. The man looked scared and he was scared, but he had been brave enough to risk his life by coming to Cole's room to give him the list of names. Cole raised his voice, "Come on, Howie. I can't do this by myself."

Howie glanced fearfully around the room. If he went with Cole and the marshal did not succeed in taking or killing Welch, then his own life wasn't worth two cents. There were enough witnesses here so that word that he'd co-operated with Cole was sure to get back to Welch.

He hesitated, thinking of the slaughter of the Indians, thinking about Salgado and Easterling. Then, impulsively, he took off his apron and came out from behind the bar.

Cole said, "Drinks are on the house, boys. Just go help yourselves." There was a sudden burst of talk, then a mass movement toward the bar.

Outside, Howie asked, voice trembling, "How can *I* help?"

"Come on across to the hotel. I want you to go up to my room. It's unlocked. The photographs are rolled up in the window shade, near the top. Get them and come on down. I'd get them myself but I don't think I could climb those stairs."

They crossed the street, and while Cole waited in the lobby, Howie went inside. Cole was thinking that, of all the men in town, Howie was the most unlikely to risk his life to help.

Howie was back in a few minutes, the photographs in his hand. He gave them to Cole, who put them into the pocket of his shirt. He didn't yet know what he was going to do. He couldn't let Nora be killed. But neither could he let Welch get away. Maybe, he thought, it would all be taken out of his hands. Maybe he'd be killed himself. He remembered what a man he'd served with in the war had said: "It's in the hands of God. I'll be hit or I won't be hit, depending on what He decides." That man had been in a lot of battles and had exposed himself repeatedly. He had never sustained a wound.

He headed toward Nora's house, Howie keeping pace. Once, Howie asked, "Can I help you?" but Cole shook his head. He was thinking about Nora, thinking that she had promised to go away with him. If anything were to happen to her now. . . .

He caught himself hurrying and forced himself to slow down, to save his leg as much as possible. Welch wasn't going to hurt Nora. Not as long as she had value to him as a hostage.

What kind of weapon would Welch have? He turned his head and glanced at Howie. "What kind of gun did he take?"

"A revolver. And the new double-barreled shotgun he bought to replace the one you smashed."

"Who's he got with him?"

"Mosely and Olivera."

They reached the alley behind Nora McKissick's house and still Cole didn't have a plan. They came up behind the stable, and Cole looked around the corner of it at Nora's back door.

The screen was closed, but the door was slightly ajar, moving back and forth slightly in the evening breeze. Through the window he could see Flagg, whom he hadn't known was there, tied to a straight-backed chair. Nora would be tied to another one, but he couldn't see her from here and he didn't dare step out into the open for fear he might be seen.

How would Welch have stationed himself and the men he had? he asked himself. Well, there would be a man in the front part of the house, in case he tried to get in that way. That would be either Olivera or Mosely, probably Olivera, because he would be the more dependable of the two.

Mosely might be in the kitchen, or he might be outside, watching and ready to let Welch know when he arrived. Welch himself was surely in the kitchen with Nora and with Flagg, the shotgun in his hands, ready to cut Cole in two the instant he came in the door.

The thing was, nobody was going to survive tonight if all did what Welch told them to. Welch wasn't going to leave anybody behind, any eyewitnesses to his murder of a U.S. marshal. He would kill Flagg, and Nora, and he might even kill Mosely and Olivera when he was through with them.

Cole turned, eased the hammer down on his gun, and handed it to Howie. "Do you know how to shoot this thing?"

"Yes sir. You thumb the hammer back, aim it, and pull the trigger."

"Think you can shoot Welch through the window and hit him, or are you shaking too bad?"

"I'm shaking, but I can steady my hands on the window jamb."

"All right, then; go around to the side of the house. There's a kitchen window there. Don't try to break the

glass and don't make any noise or he'll cut loose on you
with the shotgun. But get a bead on Welch. Nobody else."

"What are you going to do?"

"I'm going in with the photographs. I don't see what
else I can do."

"Unarmed?"

Cole nodded. "Remember, now, you shoot him the minute he raises that shotgun to take a shot at me."

"What if I don't hit him?"

"It will distract him enough so that maybe I can get to
him."

Howie said, "You're just committing suicide."

"Maybe. Anyway, if you miss him and if he gets me,
you run. Get a horse and get out of town. Get to Denver
somehow and let the marshal's office know what happened
here."

Cole took the photographs out of his pocket and gave
about half of them to Howie. Welch wasn't going to have
time to find out if all of them were there anyway. He
gripped Howie's shoulder and said, "You're a brave man."

Howie said shakily, "I sure don't feel like it."

Cole led the way out from behind the stable. He
watched until Howie had reached the kitchen window and
stationed himself there. He saw Howie nod his head to let
him know he was able to see Welch, saw Howie raise the
gun and steady it against the window jamb.

His own chest felt hollow, and there was ice in his stomach, but the tension of the moment seemed to have lessened
the pain in his wounded leg. He was going to step into that
kitchen in another moment, and the chances were good

that Welch would just blast him instantly, without saying anything or waiting for anything.

He took the remaining photographs out of his pocket. Maybe, just maybe, Welch's glance would drop for an instant to the photographs. If it did, then Howie might get a chance to shoot.

He carefully crossed the porch and opened the screen door. It squeaked.

He pushed open the back door with a shoulder and stepped inside. One hand held the fence picket, supporting him on the side where his wounded leg was. The other hand held the photographs, the picture side facing toward Welch.

Out of the corner of his eye, Cole could see Nora, face white as a sheet, eyes wide with sheer terror. Flagg looked almost equally scared, as much so as his battered face could reveal.

Welch raised the shotgun, but he hesitated the briefest instant while his glance went to the photographs. There was the bellowing sound of a shot, followed by the tinkle of broken glass cascading to the floor.

His eyes on Welch, Cole knew that Howie had missed. Welch swung the shotgun toward the window and fired instantly. The shot took out what remained of the window, and maybe hit Howie too, Cole thought, even as he put all his remaining strength into a dive at Welch's legs.

Out of the corner of his eye, he caught a glimpse of Pat Mosely in the corner, gun in hand. And suddenly, something hard and heavy and solid hit him on the shoulder; by the feel of it he knew what it was and from which direction it had come. It was his revolver. Howie had fired, and must have ducked before Welch's charge took the window out. From the ground, Howie had flung the gun in and it had struck Cole's shoulder, and now his hand groped for it and seized it by the grips.

On the floor he was, trying to bring the gun to bear. Above him, Welch, staggering from Cole's charge, was desperately trying to swing the shotgun to bear on him. Both Nora and Flagg were beyond, where they were bound to catch at least a part of the charge.

Hammer came back, muzzle steadied, and the revolver fired. The bullet must have struck Welch in the breastbone, because it drove him back as if he'd been struck by a giant fist. The shotgun discharged, but because Welch was staggering back the barrel was pointing at the ceiling. It tore a hole there big enough for a man to have stuck his arm through.

Cole knew he wasn't through. There still was Olivera and there was Mosely. But Mosely threw down his gun and raised his arms and yelled, "No! I give up! I want no more of it."

Cole yelled, "Are there any more?"

Olivera came into the kitchen, weaponless. "Fight's over," he said. "As long as Welch is dead."

Howie Bracken came in the back door. He helped Cole up, helped him to a chair. He began to work on the clothesline, untying Nora first. As soon as she was free, he began to work on Flagg.

Sheriff Thorne came through the door. Brundage was in back of him. Cole said, "Take them away. It's over. You can't protect them any longer. It has gone too far. When

G 49

they're locked up, get the others." He fished the list out of his revolver holster and handed it to Thorne.

It had seemed impossible. Now it was over; it was done. All he wanted right now was for everybody to get the hell out of there and leave Nora and him alone.

They eventually got Welch's body out. Thorne herded Olivera and Mosely toward the jail. Brundage left, his face filled with gloom as he realized that there was nothing he could do to save the reputation of the town or his own heavy investments. It was finished.

Nora studied Cole carefully. "You didn't know Mr. Flagg was here, did you?"

He shook his head. "Not at first."

"Then, you came in here like that for me?"

Uncomfortably he said, "I guess you could say that."

She came to him, and bent, and laid her soft cheek against his. "I wasn't sure, but I am now. If you'd do that for me. . . ."

She kissed him then, but lightly, because he was pale and tired and in a lot of pain. Both of them knew that there would be time, a lot of time, a whole lifetime, in fact.